Sufi

Sufi

Name Sufi
Age: 33
Ethnicity : mixed
Occupation: I cleaned out heys house But I am learning to be a social worker I don't know to be decided

About me:
My name is Sufi I was born in Romania at the age of two I was adopted in Canada but it was two years too late as I was left for dead by my mother who was a rape victim and I was tortured as a child before being adopted at age 2 year 2 months. Everything was good in Canada until I went to Catholic school that's when I ended up being tormented again even more only mentally and verbally and emotionally. I couldn't handle the stress there are some times where I wanted to end it all but I told the people that fuck off excuse my language. I ended up deciding not to hurt myself that there was gonna be some reason for me exhausting. But I ended up coming back from a shitty day at school in the seventh grade I remember them boys were really bad that day was a day in September it was a Tuesday and then what triggered my late onset PTSD was the 911 attacks that happened and I was traumatized already traumatized as it was happening again I thought this was gonna happen again to me. Only physically not just mentally or physically or emotionally. I ended up deciding to go about my life but I am not up hearing something from my mother and nearly burst in my eardrum she said bursting my right eardrum remembering this and she said you have to give back to the world I still was figuring out that when I am 33 years old and I was wondering how to get back to the world was gonna be an artist and a rapper watch I didn't know but I was I know is that I had a reason to live. High school was not that bad but I learned about Islam and became more less interested in the religion it helped me take control of my life at 8:17 when I decided to not be the bully anymore or being bullied one of the two it didn't matter I didn't want to be either I wanted to be in control of my life and I told my mother the second time to fuck off. I was not happy to say that but she had to hear it from me that I didn't care about the bullies or their existence. I excelled in high school and went on to graduate with honours it took me almost 10 to 13 years before I ended up becoming another student again in a college I'm hoping that I find what I'm looking for in life but I don't know.   I like tattoos iPhone tattoos fascinating not because I have a high pain tolerance but because they are so beautiful and intricate sometimes I thought of being a tattoo artist making people happy that way but then I ended up deciding I was going to go about writing trying to help that as well but something just wasn't right in my heart. I like astronomy a lot and most of my tattoos are astronomy related even though they're Haram in Islam. I still do the tattoos because I like the idea of being colourful and vibrant. That's just who I am. My thirst for knowledge has started when I was 16 years old when I read my first book not saying that I started to read at age 16 but I actually read my first book I wasn't big on reading as a kid except for horror and I ended up reading other types of books and then in finding out stuff about me and the world around me and I decided I was going to learn more just not just horror.   Another thing that I like to do is trick-or-treating even though I'll be doing that for the rest of my life because it's just too fucking fun is trick-or-treating I love Halloween and how fun it is to see the different designs of the pumpkins and the haunted houses is just too much for me to bear sometimes that I enjoy it. I believe there is a good scare and a healthy scare and then there's the fear that comes with the news that isn't so healthy. More on that later. I am a non-binary lesbian I was accepted as lesbian and my favourite constellation of all the 88 constellation is the Big Dipper.

Interests:
astrology, palmistry, tarot and oracle cards, Halloween, photography, Music, spirituality, philosophy, steel tongue drum, as well as tattoo design and getting tattoos myself, piercings, Shamanism, Anything esoteric will

Music:
I like everything from old country to techno and rap to metal to Horrorcore to anything else in between as well as world will I not listen to is white power bands or stupid gospel social gospel fan or a fan of white power bands my suggest finding another freaking profile to like

Movies:
Bollywood, astronomy documentaries, horror movies, Social issue movies as well as Ghibli anime is pretty good, Siren head movies on YouTube

Tv:
Grey's Anatomy, cobra Kai, Better Call Saul, various Arabic dramas, horror shows, Dr. G medical Examiner, Chicago med, Chinese dramas as well as anything foreign language and I'll watch.

Books:
Worlds most dangerous places, anything by the Dalai Lama, Shake hands with the Devil call mom myself included as an author, as well as I am interested in astronomy and astrology and whatever Esoteric books there are. And let's not for get about owly.

Heroes:
The Dalai Lama, Romeo Dallaire, my brother, and Sirenhead

Fun facts:
Member of the Facebook midnight society
Saw Sirenhead
Has three ear lobes
Two tattoos More coming
mixed race
Likes to stargaze
Urban myths and mythology believer
Smoker (quitting)
420 friendly
Atheist but spiritual

Quote: Fire in the hole bar deeply connected

Doll making or not to be

One time my brother suggested that I make dolls for a living I was thinking of that are always the only reason why I was on this planet but I didn't think that I was going to be taking courses for a social worker at the time so I didn't thanks very much and agreed to make dolls.   Are we always a good hand because of my birth father or is it I like to call an idiot number two my birth mother idiot number one. And you're gonna know why later because of what happened to me as a baby they left me abandoned because my mother was raped and then I got more or less abused in an orphanage for two years of my fucking life before being adopted so yes I was not a very happy person with my birth parents my birth Varsha protector my mother and my mother shut up protecting me the idiots I mean idiots one and idiots to. But that's gonna be another chapter. I ended up thinking because I was having idiot choose version of skills which is artistic and hand skills to maybe make a living off that I am very good with my hands usually so I thought well why the hell not I create my own tattoos anyway so I will try to make a doll even though I was afraid of fucking it up. I didn't like the audio fucking up a doll meeting screwing up the dolls face and stuff so I was very hesitant to begin with just one thing to make a tattoo for yourself or for someone else to enjoy on their skin for the rest of their life was another thing to screw up a $500 dolls face. I was not very happy about that so I didn't think very much of it.
He saw that I had a hand and let's say doll making when I was a kid in this would've been a warning signs of trauma what is it I would dismember my own Barbie dolls And then try to make sceptre actual body parts to make a super doll but I was when I was a kid I don't remember very much after like except yelled at for destroying my dolls.
When I told my mother that I was going to make dolls for a living sheet thought this wasn't a good idea because I would just screw up the dolls face make up boys or freg up or break it or whatever I usually do with dolls.   I was the a person to begin with let's just put it that way I wasn't I I was more of an action figure girl and even out that if I try to paint one forget it I was not the type of person to make toys. I remember in the third grade I was told to make a Toy out of junk which was good and fun and I was able to show it off to the class my junkie toys and I dismembered remembers again.   And trust me I had a Lotta junk so I had the biggest project to do the glue gun was always being used for that particular project I remember the kids always the other kids I mean complaining that I was hogging up the glue gun for this particular school project. But it was well worth it was a masterpiece I can't remember what it looked like but it was very interesting by no means.
And I also remember yelling at the big dipper when I was in the eighth grade wondering what the fuck I should do with my life still thinking I should do art but I was in the eighth grade. I didn't want to do art for the rest of my life I want to there was some kind of purpose in my life to help with people and Carta help with other people. People like me who were traumatized and were more or less marginalized by society. That's when I found out like the big dipper I was meant to guide people I guess that's why I have an obsession with that constellation to begin with when my father taught me how to get find the Big Dipper.   And then of course he also taught me the planets and he taught me a little bit about DNA just

enough to wet my imagination I remember when I was four years old at the time before I want to school all the school teachers from kindergarten to grade 8 had a hell of a time with me because I said oh I know what that is not interrupt the class with my knowledge about the big dipper the planet or DNA or whatever crapped in my head. So I was never really liked by the teachers. It wasn't until I was 21 years old and I found out I had an IQ of 196 one of the highest IQs. But I never told very many people that I had a very high IQ super high IQ because of my because people can be very judge mental and say no you don't have it doesn't happen that often and that kind of shit and I despise those kind of people. So I don't believe in judging people about certain things and saying oh you're crazy you're not that smart blah blah blah are you haven't seen siren head or something to those are facts. I'll tell you more about siren head and another story but right now this is just basically why I don't want to do dolls because I want to collect knowledge and me getting certificates and certification so I can actually get an actual job one day that actually involves helping people. These are things that I find that are important because I remember in the seventh grade my mother blasted my eardrum saying that I had to give back the story was is my father trying to teach me to cook in the morning which with my father usually was a disaster except with astronomy or science. I ended walking to my best friend's house at the Tom Karen BMV Karen Bambi's house was way across the fuck around town. And Karen BMV was not happy to see me she was afraid that I was going to get taken by a predator or that I was going to get killed somehow by accident or otherwise and I actually called my mother before I got home with a fucking cell phone I remember. That's why my mother said let's have a chat and then she yelled at me saying you better get back to the world you scared the shit out of me. That's when I decided I was going to give it back to the world in the hell with art. And I told my brother that the other day I cannot dude dolls because I'm afraid I'm gonna fuck up completely and fuck it up royally. I know my language is a little bit foul but you have to get used to it in this work because I am very authentic an earthy. You will find that very quickly. So to make dogs or not to make dogs that is the question the answer is forget it.

What started this was the Big Dipper

You're probably wondering where my brains a little appetite for knowledge came from it came from when I was four years old. When my father taught me about the planets and the big dipper and a little bit about DNA.   I would be there in the backyard at night in Family functions my idiot and being there with her stupid sons and my cell phone the swing set at a four just trying to figure out stuff and then my father said I'll show you something very interesting and I said watch and he said I'll show you turn me around took me out of this off the swingset turn me around pointing north inside that spoon like thing is the Big Dipper and then eight points to another store called the north star which is another which in another smaller spoon called the Little Dipper.   Enjoy face a big Gamper and little damper for quite some time that family function I never stayed up that late until I was 33 years old when I was with my brothers place entertaining some friends but anyway that's another story ion it up being amazed looking at the big Gapper it's complexity and simplicity and it's beauty it was easy on the other wasn't just easy to find but it was easy to look at it was a wonderful looking constellation to me the epitome of being Canadian. As if we lived under the big gap instead of the Maplelealea that was my opinion. So I always had another session with the big dipper and then when I was one night before school I was watching Star Trek with my father and the planet Saturn came up I said what the hell kind of plant is that even though as far as all I still had a bit of a mouse and he said that is Saturn first is mercury than Venus then where we live earth then Mars than the astroid belt Jupiter Saturn what you just saw and then Uranus Neptune and Pluto at the time I thought Pluto was a planet. It wasn't until I was an older kid or an older teen that I found out that Pluto is no longer a planet or a what is debateable as a planet. I always was interested in stuff like this. But then I also was interested in esoteric stuff when I got older but that's another story altogether. And then I remember one day I was watching Jurassic Park and they mention the three magic letters DNA and I said what is DNA and my father says the stuff that makes who you are and what you look like in the stuff. What you look like that doesn't mean diddly squat to me when I was 17 years old I was going to change that for a fact. I never really like my hair colour to begin with enc ed ask the hairdresser a colour red green or pink. That's when I decided when I was having enough of my hair colour and I was only eight years old at the time relearning the big dipper from the school when she was just embellishing on the big dipper. And I said why can I have my goddamn hair to be goddamn pink or green and they said because it's supposed to be your natural hair colour and share DNA and I said well I don't really care and then I had an obsession still at age 5 with body piercings and tattoos you know I was young was very fascinated when I saw an eyebrow ring or a nose ring or a lip ring or a nice piece of artwork on somebody's shoulder, Answer my father would get me artificial tattoos those rubber of tattoos or you rub off in the shower and they were fine but they didn't last very long and I wanted the real thing by the time I was 11 years old. That's when I ended up having a J word fight with my mother over the tattoos.

That's fine continued over 20 Audi year is 22 years when I was deciding I was going to get a tattoo she finally gave in at my age 30, and said I can get as many tattoos as I want I was wondering what the hell happened to my loving mother and who took her away from me when it was still her nonetheless and I was wondering why was all I being told one minute I couldn't get a tattoo in the next minute you can get a tattoo or as many as you want and I was very sure there was an alien that took over my mothers body. But it wasn't an alien it was just her being her loving self. I am not being sarcastic and this is my adoptive mother next chapter will be about my first true shitty years of my life and then where I came to be and how I became a Canadian citizen and stuff so stay tune for that. But anyway she was a very good mother I ended up one day at age 33 getting a tattoo of a Jupiter not just because I called her the pearl the size of Jupiter but also because I Ended up with a brother who was very good with astronomy as well his name is Ryan and my father was the one that taught me the plan is a big difference so forth when I was a tiny child so therefore the Jupiter what is a masterpiece for everyone in my family.   And I also remember that the six grade and I know this sounds like gibberish right now telling you about random memories but I remember seeing a university like textbook a picture of a water molecule with pink hydrogen atoms in an Blue oxygen atom has the word H20 I finally learned won the Hardaway h2no. But that'll be a different story on on the last because that's a long bastard of a story that I really wish I could block out but I can't because I have the memory of a super computer or an iPad one of the two and he cannot wipe it really easily. There are sometimes I go around my group home and I see something I would I said I wish I didn't see that I wish I can and see that I'm not gonna say exactly what but I'll just say there are some things that I see and there are some things that I on wish I could unsee. And there was a lot of things I wish I could erase from my brain or my eyes memory as well my eyes even have memories and sometimes they come back when you go to sleep seeing someone having a shit or something so I wasn't too fun there I said it. But that wasn't that's just the bad part that's only one bad part about living where I was living in a group home after and this is another bastard of a story how I want to live in a group home. And how I ended up learning what I learned anyway so there you go.

On humanity

You're probably wondering why I started with Winston Churchill's all the humanity because this is gonna be the really bastardy part of my story my beginning the genesis of my life and the genesis of my PTSD. The picture of them all. OK idiot number one name Tintin Mustafa ended up getting raped by my idiot number two father who had good hands always go to his hands apparently and then she gave birth to me didn't wanna have anything to do with me a quarter in my friends and family and I can tell she didn't really want very much to do with me because she supposedly "" gave me up for adoption but was more or less leaving me for dad because I was a product of rape. She hated my God and she wanted nothing more with me except for me to be shipped off to an orphanage if that is if I survive the first day on a cold table. Then the shit really started to hit the fan when I was pulling in the orphanage when I was there I was 30 kids to a room and more or less 30 brats to a room. All screaming and yelling all yelling and screaming in your name and throwing shit around and other gross stuff. It was during the chucheschu reign of the idiot country I call Romania. Again don't ask me how to spell is that jack ass his name because I'm telling you he was horrible. He had an obsession with trying to make the country like China with so many damn children it wasn't even funny regularly he liked boys so he can get them in the secret police that's what I was told but my memory was shit being thrown around rats in a room 30 of them screaming at me and I'm probably was screaming at them too. But then the hard part was the idiots dictator ended up being overthrown and then why don't you have a Civil War if I remember my worlds most dangerous places by Robert Young Powlton that usually these

things invite terrorists particularly Islamic terrorists are just terrorist in general who wanna start up even more of a shit show.
And for me they started a shit show even more so for me than anything else they were causing a lot of problems in my birth country ruining everything and I know who they were they were Al-Qaeda. My least favourite people in the world the real idiot so I find. Why do I say the radiance because if you hurt a woman or child you're a fucking idiot to me nothing more than a clown why should I be afraid of you. But I was afraid of them when I was a baby because this is what they were doing to me and I'm sorry I'm gonna have to say trigger warning......... torture They did everything from waterboarding stress positions to starvation isolation cold and hot and as far as pulling out fingernails and sleep deprivation I was not a happy kid and soon I ended up being having my hair yanked out and you name it it was the worst thing on the planet. I know this is disturbing but I have to tell you what these fucktard's dead to me and these Al-Qaeda fuckers. I was not happy and I'm sorry to use this kind of language but and tell you what they did to me but that's what they did and they probably did more I'm pretty sure I can feel a sensation that I'd rather not feel. That means I may have done more than just the typical torture stuff but that I'll never know for sure I do remember being water boarded and being left in very odd positions a.k.a. stress positions and being isolated and starved until I was nearly dead and then of course it was sleep deprivation they were they were using that to piss me off in other words torture. And I was just newborn until I was two years two months.
Find the time I was adopted and I say it was two years too month too fucking late I added up the siding yeah I was gonna have a the pain tolerance even though I was a tar or at the time of a nice degree black belt because I was anticipating nothing but pain so you may as well pucker up. And then I was adopted in Canada.. My parents had a fight with my two idiots says I call my birth parents I don't know about my birth father if he was mine or not but still had a fight with that jack ass to. In the next thing you know I ended up having my records destroyed not just by the terrorists but also by the fucking authorities so my parents can adopt me and my name which was Sufi Mustafa was destroyed that was my birth certificate and then put an ashtray and burned. Then they were able to get me in to the airport and then I was thought I was Scott free. Why it wasn't like that the pain still continued why because I had to get my fucking shots. Like any other kid I didn't like getting a needle. And I was it the usual three-year-old to 18-year-old response to getting a flu shot or whatever you needed to get in the school it was just a pain in my shoulder and I didn't pucker for that sucker. Because I thought I was safer in that country and then soon enough when I was able to learn how to talk and walk and I was a little delayed at the time because of the freaking torture I ended up being pulled in to get this and this is the most stupid thing I've ever been put in new was daycare. I thought I was being a Bandan and that the terrorists were going to come back to haunt me and torture me again so I ended up going into survival mode and beating up most of the kids and taking their food. This kind of abuse lash until I was at least nine years old and I said I have had it. But anyway I didn't was not very like in daycare and then I found out the most stupidest thing why I was putting the daycare......... Social skills to help me build social skills for school and it took me six years do you get it through my parents thick heads that this was not her way of trying to teach social skills in fact this is a way of making a criminal out of your daughter. It took so many times that they had to say oh she had a pissy day at kindergarten she had a pissy day at this program and then that was the end of that and I just had to go to school. But it was a very horrible experience for me I remember punching one kid in kindergarten I was dress for years older at the time in the nose breaking his nose the blood was gushing and he was because he was taking one of my fucking cookies. Yes I was that strong and it didn't hurt my little fast when I was that age to go after another kitty was eating my candies or my cookies. So I decided my pain tolerance was more than that of a horse or a 90 Dan black belt and I was wondering why.
I still consider daycare to be kiddy prison or a kiddy Guantánamo to me because of why I was thrown in there and the approximation of when I was adopted made a

Canadian citizen and then turned into daycare and I was freaked out shit less. I was not a very happy camper until I was around 13. It was just a sound on the goddamn daycare was reminiscing of that of the orphanage except I was not being tortured but I was in survival mode so I just was anyone who looked at my food got the fast. And I was as far as I can and I was very underweight and very supposed to be very weak and very stupid but I wasn't. So it didn't turn out the way the doctors want it to turn out me being very weak and very yeah damn let's put it that way. Instead I was just a slow process it took me 33 years to get to where I wanted in life. But the weak part I learned and taught them that I was not weak and then I saw the doctors were dumbasses. And when was in grade can I found out that doctor just one more than the masses they were horrible human beings.

Kindergarten and the word

You can chill off the bath that it was a very big mistake for my parents to put me in Catholic school let alone school instead of homeschooling because here's the reason why. I get home from school my mom asked me over dinner and this is Sammy funny and not so funny at the same time and I asked answer her question what did I learn today and I said motherfucker yeah the big MF word I said it in front of my father he choked on his dinner I remember that and then the next hours later he is all right side went limp he had a headache his face wasn't moving very well and there was other things that I learned one hour signs of a stroke yeah slurred speech he had the lamb side of his face and he was normal on one side that was basically what it was. Wasn't that bad that word yes it was and why did I learned that fucked up word, Catholic school particularly first day of kindergarten from a brat named Mitchell White. I remember Mitchell white very well that he would always be swearing all the time and he would always let off the F bomb and let off the MF motherfucker bomb, he made violent J of the Insane Clown Posse sound like the Dalai Lama and I learned a lot from him as far as swearing was concerned and let me tell you a thing or two about swearing. It's like the aids virus once you get it you got it for life you're screwed. And it's more infectious then aids virus, why because it was very easy to catch by listening and memorizing the damn swearwords that this kid was leading a rap and he was literally saying every word and it's airborne this disease called swearing in potty mouth. And just like the aids virus which is not which is more blood-borne the swearing virus is more or less airborne and you're stuck with it as well for life just like the aids virus six Apple one is blood-borne the other is more or less airborne or to the ear. Anyway I remember my father being in the hospital for at least a month for a friggin stroke that I caused or I remember causing at the time or thinking I caused by saying motherfucker. And that's when I tried to stop swearing but as I said I found out it was like a disease chronic disease once you have it you got it for the rest of your life. And I would periodically swear at times and then would stop and then start up again and then stop it would just be like flareups another disease like a rash sometimes they come and go. It was just horrible and when my father was in the hospital I remember him he couldn't talk he was weaker than supposedly I was and he hadn't had use of his right side or whatever side was numb. Then he had to learn how to speak and walk again if I remember correctly then he started to become more prone to TIAs or mini strokes later on in his life that I and I feel like I was the one that kind of buggered up his health.

So let this parent be a lesson do not bring your kids if they have a chronic Pottymouth do not send them to a public or Catholic school for other kids to learn their foul language just homeschool them or have the other kid be homeschooled either way their shit shouldn't be happening in there I said it. It was just horrible very dirty habit that I couldn't get out of even 33 years of age now I still try to get out of that habit and I cannot get out of that habit because it's so fucking hard with the news and the idiots that people idiotic things people do in the idiotic Warren Ukrainian stuff and the genocide and stuff that are going on on this planet that I can't help it but I swear.

Now I wanna say this I really let a rep dipper after the 9/11 attacks and I don't usually wanna blame a terrorist attack for bad behaviour but that's when I really started saying fuck off and fuck you and all those lovely terms because why and I hate to use this as an excuse but it was PTSD late onset PTSD childhood PTSD. Seeing those goddamn towers crumble and fall in those people die all 3000 of them die was just horrible enough to bring back the memories of the fucking orphanage and my war zone and I was in seeing the different Warzone's in the newsreels as well as sing a song I've been long again was just horrible and then I just couldn't stop the swearing right off the bat I just said oh fuck there's that fucking clown again and then that's when I couldn't stop F bombing no pun intended but I was just F bombing everywhere I go in Louisiana F bomb fuck this fuck that it was horrible. And I it took me 20 years 21 years and I'm still learning not to say the F bomb or the F word actually to be more exact I'm not trying to be inconsiderate of the 3000 people that died on 911 but I'm just saying that the F bomb was some thing I use a lot fuck fuck fuck fuck fuck fuck fuck fuck fuck fuck fuck fuck that's all I was saying every second freaking word it wasn't until I was in the eighth grade one I was addressed then I had a very bad potty mouth and that I was starting to have flashbacks nightmares and behaviors. Particularly the behaviours were me yelling and screaming and swearing at the other students not because I was around other children jet just because I was being an asshole I thought at the time and I had to be going into counseling. They missed diagnosed me with Asperger's which was a real bad move. Because people with Asperger's are genuinely happy go lucky people and I'm usually I go fuck yourself piss off person. It wasn't until I was around 18 or 19 when I read the book by Romeo Dallaire shake hands with the devil when I realized that I actually had laid on sad childhood PTSD because I was able to relate to him more than Rain Man he was a lucky Slappy happy son of a bitch. So I was wondering one of the mysterious behaviours the mysterious flashbacks and the Rangers and nightmares were coming from and when I read shake hands with the devil I was able to realize this was who I was but it didn't happen to find me at all. Instead I was going to fight it by first getting the right diagnosis. even if I had to kick my parents car and dent it.   Oh I remember that day with my father that I could not he told me I was a little I'm not gonna say this particular word in the story but he was really really enthusiastic and I think it was the C word he used as an even a wart and he said you little you know wart you kicked indent the car I don't want you in my house I told him to shut the fuck up and then I didn't wanna listen to his whining then my mother started to cry and said she has something really seriously wrong with her and is an aspirin nurse and then I ended

up going to the doctor the same day and I got off my ADHD medication was told I had PTSD laid on South and that I was to take certain medication for my PTSD I ended up developing also insomnia as well as other horrible things. That's one things got a little rough between me and my family. Was I going to be one of the homeless youth at or around this lovely planet that had to leave because her mental health and her relationships with her parents or shit no I just was going to make a statement out of the ass I think you're really saying I ain't leaving they were going to leave or I was going to willingly go to a group home one day. And that's why it happened one day was my mom ended up having an online affair behind my fathers back, The poor bastard had dementia at the time what really made me sad and then he ended up deciding he was going to be yelling and screaming and having behaviours like anyone with dementia and I was very sad for him and I feel sorry for the son of a gun my own father wasn't the most perfect human being according to my brother but anyway we ended up in it up standing up for my father the guy that my mother was having an online affair was got this ISIL, and I don't know how many fucking times I told my mother that this guy was a jihadist piece of shit and then I wasn't gonna have this in my house. I got so bad me trying to get enough and my father that I had to leave the house after my mother nearly died of drinking why she was drinking because Mr. ISIL was actually telling her to drink and don't get me started on this I don't wanna even start on this but I ended up going to a nice group home where I ended up making my niece and was able to spread my wings.
It took me two years the whole pandemic of COVID-19 to talk to my mother again and then rekindle our relationship she had to apologize it took me a long time to forgive her on that one.

H2No: memory

H2O or H2No.   Well it's the louder because well what happened was when my mother met the ice sky we had a flood in our fucking house. And I remember those very correctly that I remember seeing the ceiling burst where is the water coming down all over the fucking living room and I said motherfucker for the second time in my life that I remember where I can't remember completely what I had said over the years of my 30 years at this time but I know I was like mother fucker the water is out of the ceiling and my parents watching this certain Sufi watch your language. Well how can I watch my goddamn language what I'm seeing the goddamn ceiling fall apart like well why can't cookie at a daycare centre and then hang up splashing water all over my shit my favourite hats my favourite books some of my books had to be destroyed because of mould and then I found out we had a live in a motel for three months which was a God awful experience. This is one this gets a little hairy with a mental health. And I'll admit I got a little hairy. I ended up every time my mother yelled at me at the instruction of the iso guy that she would really say demeaning things to me and then I would end up having to hear voices in my head,

yes I have ended up hearing voices in my head because I couldn't handle hearing my mother being somebody she wasn't. She was really out of her whack out of her job on this and she was not herself this is one of the girl I was getting into her brain like a earwig and the one year she was really horrible at that time and was drinking starting to drink heavily and she would just let it rip on me. And in the next you know I have a mental break down and I'd start hearing demonic voices. But that wasn't the end of that soon I ended up having prophetic dreams of the war in Ukraine the Covid camps in India as well as what is going on with east Turkestan and Tibet I knew about the bad but not about east Turkestan my ancestral homeland. And I was also given a tour of hell one night as well as seeing other disturbing things like prophecies and other things I was only 30 years old and I was a prophetess. But someone would consider me a little whack job because of the demonic voices I heard I only heard the demonic voices the one time on my mother wouldn't shut her gob. So I would train the demonic voice is just a shut it up. She soon found out that she could trigger me and this is at the hands of this ISIS guy and I remember this guys name was Mohamady Stefan of Ilboudo.
And I remember a lot about the seeing angels this was not psychosis this time after a while I ended up having past life flashbacks that I haven't had since I was four years old and I'll get to that another time but anyway I ended up having flashbacks where I was imam Shamil, Among other places in the geographic region I was on mass I Warrior dream time in Australia a Inuit shaman and all sorts of things. I didn't know that I was either not my main past lives but they were my secondary or tertiary reincarnations. My main parish lies I know were samurai ninja as well as Buddhist monks and then I found out when I was visiting my brother I was also a Brahman, as the highest caste in the Hindu castes system and I was an astronomer. Why do I know this because I have an obsession with astronomy to begin with because of my father he kick started the obsession and other little things that were very a Brahmin like. So I ended up being a modern-day Brahman. And I found out that I was more or less A Brahman because of my interest in my past life as well le Vedic astronomer.
It was unusual to find that out but anyway Leah that's this whole shit show with the guard for Makino faster on the terrorist and my father's dementia made everything toxic so I had to live in a group home where I live now and I ended up deciding I was going to go and spread my wings. But not before deciding to get the Burkina Faso terrorist to face what he did and he didn't take it very well I remember it this very well and there's my car some nightmares for you. I called him to see you were and told him to stay away from my mother and that he was making a stray from my father in marriage and that he was ruining everything. And then he was like c word terrorist and nothing more than to faker poser trying to be a Muslim Then I ended up deciding I was going to say the c word once again to him. He decided he was going to threaten me with the most horrific torture there ever was and I told him to bring it on and that he was a pile of shit. I said if you your people trying to torture me once before yes and failed they are not going to succeed again and basically told him to go fuck him self on Facebook I remember that exactly it was an April day I was just getting my shit from my house to my group home and I remember him being a little shit on my Facebook messenger. It was not my finest moment but I had to do this for my father and myself and for the fact that my mom was nearly dying. So I was not very happy about that at the time I was considered homeless at the time because I was you know where I was going to live or the people that were coming to support me didn't know where I was going to live until I ended up coming around with a smile on my face every day and actually behaving properly instead of like a little shithead. She had had being a little brat meaning I was actually starting to grow up and think straight for once in my life I just had to get out of work very toxic environment. That's why I need a saw it I was going to stay until I wore myself out and I haven't wore myself out yet.

DNA testing: memory
Before the asshole from Burkina Faso and before the flood I remember wanting to get my DNA test and I wanted to get the ancestry DNA test to find out why I was actually Uighur and Tibetan anything else by any chance. I remember it was $180 the same amount of money as my first tattoo but anyway I'll get to the first tattoo later anyway I ended up buying the card off of ancestry.ca. And I found out some interesting stuff about three or four months later and I was also Uighur Tibetan Bhutani and Indian as in East India, Siberian the various stands and Pakistan and Afghanistan and Iran as well as Arab and Chechen as well as white. I remember this was still when my mother was a decent person she was at the time I steal a Ni in person she's a niece in person now but I had a coer shit out of her but anyway she said OK we got a multicolour daughter she said I remember hearing that completely well and I was glowing. And soon pretty soon I end up buying stuff that had a lot of colour and it will be closing or otherwise if it had a lot of colour I would buy it and use it for us to make myself to say I hey I'm multiracial I meant multicultural multi coloured if you would. I've never been so proud in my proud of my idiot one an idiot too for the first time in my life I've never been so proud of my birth parents so this is where I was physically strong and physically flexible as well as I was a stubborn ass human being as well. And I was very happy every day they would come up with a different ethnic group and I would say well that explains it. And it was getting to the point where am I DNA results started lighting up like a Christmas tree particularly around Asia not so much around here but I was given Balkans and Ukraine and Romania but never very much in the Europe department I was more or less in Asia. And this is it going to be a funny story that happened a few days ago in my group home that wasn't too funny at first. Because I was more or less Asian my DNA and my hair was thicker than all hell I ended up trying to do a pixie cut or redo a pixie cut because I was trying to shave my not shave my head but do a pixie cut with the house cutters and I broke the cutters by accident because my hair was so goddamn thick. I remember calling my adoptive mother the one that I had a get an apology out of her being drunk and everything and saying listen my birth mother is dead meat why because I broke the clippers. Boy was I angry when I wrote the clippers at the group home because they weren't mine to break and besides I don't like breaking things especially with my own fucking hair. I told the workers and they said life happens when I said this is still embarrassing for me that my hair broke the clippers I never saw the clippers again and it was just a few days ago and I haven't seen the clippers again nor do I wanna ever see them again I want to see a new pair of them because I'm pissed still. My hair is like Mongolian horse hair emphasis on Mongolian why because I am Mongoloid Asian.
From Kabul to Iran to xi'an china to Lasha tibet to Mumbai India to Kabul Afghanistan and Turkestan Kazakhstan I was full-blown mongoloid except for my hair facial features instead of my facial features being fully Asian they were a mixture of Asian Arab and white some people would consider me a guy they some people have actually miss gendered me because of my ancestry and I have told him that they are nothing more than motherfucking racist another time I said motherfucker but this time I was warranted because I hate racism and I have been called chink another horrible stupid stuff that I don't like very much and I've been called a guy and I was also told that I was a guy one really I know better when I go to the bathroom and female. So I said that's it I've had enough of these miss rendering racists and that they are going to bite the wind more or less and I said that they were going

to have an end one day because of their behaviour because there's a lot of mixed race people out there whether they be black and white or whatever or white and indigenous or Y in Spanish or whatever there's so many different kind of people. I just have to have the most ass in the groups in my DNA and it shows in my face and sometimes people either see me as beautiful or they see me as but ugly either way I don't really give a shit I call the people call me but ugly racist pricks. And I flew from the bird right away and I have decided not to bother with them. I decide I am a Jamila or a good looking person of beautiful. And I continue to see myself as the queen and beautiful and regal an elegant because that's what I was in the Han dynasty was a Uighur princess. And if anyone told me otherwise and I was not supposed to be good looking because of my race usually got a fist in their face anyway because and I don't usually go with discrimination with violence but in this case I am too proud of my own heritage and I despise being bullied. I remember one time as well when I was in grade 80 this is their favourite in Catholic school after 911 or horrible names derogatory Muslim names and then there is also spazz out and retard. The Muslim name is because of the way I look just physically and because the 9/11 attacks just happen spazzing out because of my PTSD and retard because I had a different way of viewing things in the world. Either way I didn't like it and one time one kid hit all three faces search the derogatory word for a Muslim and the Spazzout and the retard words as well and I was going through PMS and I saw him in the face that was the end of my Spazzout career if you word. Because the principal saw me as a bully and as a threat and decide he was going to threaten me with everything from juvenile prison Juvie to adult prison to Guantánamo to Abu Ghraib to even renditions and Bagram he was hateful man. And I remember I was coming home one day and my mom listed out the presents that she was more or less hearing about from the principal and she said you're going in a martial arts whether you like it or not do you know not know that the martial arts is going to take over most of my high school career and that I was going to end up being more or less Japanese mafia and I was not pulling shit legs or pulling chains I was not Jankin change or anything the sensei that was teaching me martial arts was unusually nice and then when I was which is very weird at a yellow belt ended up going to a tournament and then after that I was wild everyone in the tournament even the black belts and then the next thing you know I was told I was supposed to be yakuza. And that's one intense and 11th grade I ended up seeing some Sadie looking Japanese guys going around my person or going around my school or neighbourhood I was not very happy and had to quit martial arts because of not that reason just that reason but because I also ended up having another flareup with PTSD and that's the next chapter.

Writing

I remember before my seventeenth Birthday that I was given my first book of poetry by my father and it was his old high school poetry book that he used to read for school. When he was my age this is when I started going through my first depression. And this is what ultimately got me to be reverting to Islam in the first place. Was this poetry mark. It wasn't Islamic poetry was just general poetry what time I ended up going to my neighbours house to get some gauge steel rings like the ear expanders or flash expanders for your ears and I was talking to mother as a girl was getting her flesh expanders the ear gauges, and I saw a Koran and some Islamic poetry and I ended up liking what I saw I ended up wanting to learn more than what the school was teaching me what was the negative side of Islam. I ended up learning more about it that it was a more fast growing religion it was mostly popular in Asia Middle East and Africa and some parts of Europe particularly my part of Europe that I was born as well. And then I slowly learn more about these different cultures in Asia Middle East Africa and Europe like Bosnia Chechnya and other places and I wanted to learn more about these places this is what this one stupid rat Rady poetry book from my father dead and then what happened was is that as I was reading up on Islam and reading the Quran and reading Islamic poetry I found that my depression started to lift up and I was able to feel better about myself it wasn't because of the medication I was on which was Prozac it was because I was learning about some thing that was bigger than myself and I was being happy for the first time in my life. Did I wear the hijab no but I did pray five times a day facing my car and I also was very careful about how I ate I try to avoid meats still do to this day. And that righty tidy book that my father gave me inspired me to write books I remember when I was 30 years old I was always reading books whether they be Islamic or otherwise and I would be reading and reading and reading and then soon enough I found out about Wordpad. Hey social writing platform where you can actually Published your own stories I don't get up writing my own story which was my autopsy which wasn't based on anything of my life but it was based on my nightmares that I've had plenty of times why because when I was in the 10th grade it before I had my first depression and reverted to Islam I ended up finding out that doctors were horrible to the Asians in the holocaust as well as the Jewish people my Jewish brothers and sisters not just my Asians but also to the Jew my Jewish brothers and sisters and some of my Christian brothers and sisters I was really horrified and I said those fucking bastard better not try it on me. And I've always had a rhetoric against doctors. Why because I think they're racist sons of bitches in my massage that I was that's what got me writing in the first place was my autopsy what I wrote and then I ended up deciding that I was going to write to lessen the effects of my PTSD. So I use WordPad a lot. I ended up using WordPad a lot and getting a lot of followers I ended up writing a different bunch of topics yakuza or as much as my mental health, and islam. I know I was proud of my writing pretty soon when I ended up going to the group home I ended up taking a webinar with a published author I asked him and this was on zoom if I wanted how would I go about to self publish a block he said why not try Rocky Ken doll direct publishing so I looked up the rocky site which is a shopping site. And then I looked up Rocky Kindle direct publishing. And then the way I go after the webinar was over I publish my first book of poetry what does non-Islamic I think it I can't remember the name of the book but I know it was on my legal name. What are the Sufi Nelson. So word pad was gonna be used as a aircraft carrier for my books to go on to Rocky Kindle direct publishing. And I ended up finding out that this was fun actually publishing these things for money and I was very happy I started riding even more than I usually did. It helped a lot even more because I was able to reach more people about my PTSD about my story and other stuff is very interesting I even did dream journals journals and other stuff and I posted them on Rocky Kindle direct publishing. It didn't take too long to get to the use and knowledge of the Kindle direct publishing and I was able then pretty soon do use D to the draft2digital not to be misconstrued worse dungeons and dragons but it was draft2digital. And then pretty soon my books ended up going on Apple as well as many other great book sites for your e-books I started off with e-books and then pretty soon when I was progressing with my writing ended up with got this paper backs and then soon enough hard covers I had a heart few hard covers Published as well. So that's how I dealt with my PTSD and then I also from Rocky I also ended up buying a steel tongue drum. That was the very first instrument I learned and I learned real fast not because I had to but because it was just so interesting the sounds and I would play it and then pretty soon a year later I ended up learning how to play it completely differently the correct way the spiritual way and now everyone can find it very relaxing. I'll tell you more about the rest of this another time about how I'm going to end up in a talent show. But anyway it's because I am went on YouTube to go and learn how to use a hand pan which I never got but I ended up also learning how to use the steel Toungedrum. Which is the dome like sang and you walked the "tongs with your cut out and you make a nice sound with them and you can experiment with the sounds and they help with my PTSD as well it started off with PTSD trying to get rid of it and then it started off well yes easy just drew and I ended up learning more about my capabilities as a musician and pretty soon I ended up learning from a celebrity the guitar and then very soon after that the ukulele. And I am not joking about this particular celebrity her name is Amanda Johnson. Just look it up on Botify and you'll find out what I mean. I ended up also finding out that I was able to wrap after I ended up with COVID-19 one time never went to the hospital never even had a use the halls Lasic but I was able to adequately sang but gave up on singing and ended up starting the rap and now I have two rap albums one coming out one already out that has a lot of foul language so I might make it famous there.

Rap and education

I met this guy name Christopher he was one of the workers at my group home he taught me how to rap properly and I soon was going above his head with the wrapping I even have my own true tube channel which was very interesting. Where I would wrap about my thoughts and interests in my feelings and what's going on in the world and stuff some people would say that that would be depressing stuff but I was actually more to educate people about PTSD was like to have PTSD what's going on in the world my prophecies and stuff that's how I delivered everything with the rap and writing. My rapper name is Sufi Spraggah bint Mustafa, on Lafayette and there I was allowed to go after I used amuse the app to distribute my music and I was able

to post myself every 21 days to tell my story to wrap. But with Christopher I was also starting to get a sense of my orgasm in touch with my thirst and hunger and greed for knowledge not greed and not in a bad way but just in a way of saying that I was hungrier than I siren head I'll tell you about siren head later. Which he has a hat hell of an appetite I'll tell you that much but not as much as my brain.
I started asking do you know anything Anything about online free courses for careers and I said I was very interested in learning about different stuff from psychology to psychiatry to mental health do anything that'll help me get out in the world and also what I deem interesting. And pretty soon I ended up learning about that these programs like the homelessness learning hub.   The first thing I learned was a course called use reconnect and that I ended up learning more about well not tru about myself what about you with whole lessness and how I can turn into chronic homelessness and I can be caused by anything from substance abuse mental health or not getting along with my parents something that rang through to me because I had a mental health problem my mother had a substance-abuse problem particularly alcoholism at one point when I pissed off out of the house and I wasn't getting along with my father very well either so either way I could've been very I was lucky that I was in the house that I am now in the group home or else I probably will be in my ass on the street being exposed to a culture of things that are not very positive that say like substance abuse and other horrible stuff that I wouldn't want to put up with personally or experience personally let's say.
The course was supposed to take three hours it took me an hour to get the course done and two hours to get the damn quiz right. But I took a long time for the quiz and after the quiz was done I downloaded my first certification certificate and I was very happy and hyper and I still lamb to this day and now I am very excited with what that's going to bring next. And I'm going to learn more different courses on the site. And also I discovered that I also found another app not with the help with Christopher but with the help of myself and the App Store con learning where I learned about where I'm learning more in depth about astronomy in-depth meaning like with numbers and stuff like a year with the astronomical unit and stuff like that and there is Nanometers and stuff like that which are very interesting and then I'm learning about the different stars different kind of stars blue Giants white giants red Giants and stuff like that man sequenced stars orange stars brown stars you name it there is all over the place. And that's why I started off and then I ended up leaving to go grocery shopping one day came back Christopher was there and he said what's your email I said well something something at gmail.com, and he gave me the course link to the homelessness learning hub and that's when I ended up deciding I'm going to not do art for a living right instead I was going to help people and garden people kind of like the big dipper that's what I was gonna do for the rest of my life and that's what I was going to do I said it was a commitment that made itself because it was bound to happen because it was the things I went on with my life and I'm gonna continue on tell you more things about my life this hasn't this life was a connect the dots it was not something that was random like most people lives a random my life was more or less connect the dots and everything happen for a reason even the bad stuff and I realize that I was meant to have in life experience to help people. And I was honoured for the first trying to have my little piss off called PTSD what is it in the social work world is a blessing not a piss off. I just started the first I just did the first youth connect course and I'm going to start doing more courses as the days go on not weeks and I'll still be working on my astronomy. I am very interested in the world around me and I'm very happy that I'm going to be able to partake in it not just be on disability and be feeling sorry for myself. That is for wimps to feel sorry for yourself and to be on disability unless you're actually disabled then you can be on this is ability but if you have a good IQ decent working body I don't see why you should be on that damn stuff except to get money and I don't believe in getting money for the sake of getting money so I want to support my society and want to work and partake and that's what it was and I remember one time on my mother signed me up for ODSP that I was not very happy I was pissed off and she said you're going

on disability pension because of your whatever was going on in my head at the time and I was madder than a hornet I said I didn't want this I want to make a living and make a career out of my life and make a good choice instead but she had her way anyway and I was on disability and I'm trying to get off the damn thing now they ODSP. My mother derailed my future for a little bit I could've been something a lot more but now I can be something a lot more because I got out of a sticky situation. I remember one dream I had an issue come in the next chapter.
You remember that I pray five times a day. But I also A punk goth emo girl, so I always wear different hair colours usually every day with a different way because of my damn hair tie Mongoloid I cannot go around with hair dye and bleach all the time so I bought some wigs. And I ended up the song I like wings better than dying my fucking hair so that was beside the point. So I machine girl and a believer in lucid dreaming and one time this is what happened..........

Lucid dreaming

OK you know I have nightmares because of my fucking PTSD right well when I had a mental health worker she told me about lucid dreaming and trying to keep a dream journal. I also was reading a book on esoteric shamanism and spirit animals I have three spirit animals are actually the peacock bird, the bat, the wolf. And I was also learning about in this esoteric shamanistic book that you are they learn lucid dreaming so I learned lucid dreaming very much so and started practising I would plan implant an idea in my head like I would with a Bork and start off with that and then go to sleep and watch the dream happen instead of having a fucking nightmare. Well this is going to be a weird story to tell you and some of you might find this a little crazy. But you know I am Muslim revert but anyway I ended up having a dream around Halloween where I ended up having this dream where I was talking with a Prophet Muhammad (saw) he said that my dreams and parents were going to come true and then I had a purpose in life to help other people. I still remember the stream even though it was two years ago it was very inspiring and a little offputting but very inspiring to notice that one of my ancestors told me to help other people. And there was through Lulu dreaming and Dominic books that I was reading and I was very grateful that I was able to meet the profit of my religion in the first place peace be upon him. And I learned that there are plenty of people that need help I didn't know how I was going to go about fulfilling this dream and fulfilling the profits wish for me until I met Christopher and then I ended up learning about these different courses first on the khan Academy for astronomy and then I blossomed a mouse another sciences and then I ended up learning other things and then soon enough on that side Khan Academy and then I ended up learning about social issues and social work through the courses I'm now taking through the homelessness learning hub and I'm learning other certifications to help me get along in life and help people as well.

Do I still Do art I just don't do drawings on dolls for my brother that's all I'm saying is that I don't doll art more or never get doll art and never will do doll art.

Instead I ended up deciding to design cartoons for the tattoo artist that did my second tattoo I'll tell you about my first tattoo in a minute but the second tattoo was an astronomy relayed one which was a Jupiter with them and Dela design on it and then I also got some semicolons on my middle fingers why on my middle finger is because there are a lot of assholes I'll tell you to go kill yourself and some people actually go ahead and take their advice "advice" and it's very sad and I've been told that many times by these assholes that I should go kill myself plenty of times sometimes I was very close to doing this or going through with the thought when I was in my early 20s and I said fuck this this is not worth my energy or time or whatever else that is more valuable than racking myself and checking myself so I ended up getting tattoos of semicolons on my middle fingers and if someone says I'm ugly or something they get the finger and then they'll see that on my middle finger that I have the semicolon and that I cannot be struck down by words or mean thoughts or actions I was going to be letting my story live on and Miles story will live on for the rest of my life that's one set of tattoos the other was the Jupiter which was for my mother father and brother we are all interested in astronomy except for my mother I called her the Jupiter pearl which is the pearl the size of Jupiter. So that's why the Jupiter. I remember showing my brother my the original Jupiter design he ragdoll Annette meaning he really yeah he harassed me about it and I said well it's just a tertiary design the artist is going to do the actual cleaning up of the damn thing. And then I actually showed him the tattoo after it was done he was surprised that I was able to create tattoos. But not as surprised as the artist who did the tattoo and did the semicolon tattoos as well. I ended up having a semi-job still do have a semi-job trying to create tattoos for people that might be interesting for the artist to work on other people. I have 10 or 11 so far done and I just have to do a few more and then I can send them off to the artist to see if he would be interested in the artwork. I am very honoured about this and I don't know what might happen after this this is also a little bit of a job I also have a job working for tattoos cleaning add a day program and I clean like a son of a bitch I clean like there's no tomorrow and I clean as if I mean it. And I clean thoroughly very well clean and disinfect everything. That's at hey house. I am paid $20.10 bucks an hour two hours and I do it very well and sometimes I do other little knickknacks around the house the group home just to get some more padding for the tattoos. The next tattoo will be of a big dipper inside the moon which is on my neck and some esoteric designs for my knuckles which is very interesting for me I don't know how much this will cost but I have to wait until September to actually verbalize that I want to do this. But my first tattoo that got me going was the swearing water molecule and I did that because of my fucked up relationship with water that's why the water molecules swearing and I named it Spanky. He's on my right shoulder the Jupiter is on my left bicep and I'm planning on getting more tattoos neck down. I am very interested in tattoos and piercings the piercings we have a little bit of a problem with it because I was an idiot enough to try to pierce myself and you know I'm a great study I'm a little quick study learned it off YouTube and then the next thing you know I did one piercing wrong which was the medusa and that was the end of it I ended up in the hospital with a mini staff infection if you well and I ended up having to give up on piercings or at least do it yourself piercings and I said there's no fucking way I'm doing this again so when I got the tattoo done professionally I just tired I'm going to have my piercings done professionally and then I was going to be able to take care of these things a lot easier in the long run if they're done professionally as I did with Spanky and the Jupiter and my semicolon tattoos everything was very well taken care of after it was done professionally all I have to do is make up the design in a way I go make the money and go to the tattoo parlor. iPhone getting tattoos is a way of helping my self heal through whatever, I want to well I shouldn't say whatever I know what trauma I went through and it was a lot of trauma. It's normal Asakusa

Mercedes women's just trying to use art to express who I am just like wearing a wig or wearing make up or wearing jewellery or whatever I also have other means of healing myself like crystals and crystals like healing crystals Reiki and also my medication. I'll tell you about Reiki pretty soon when I decide to tell you and there are some funny stories with this.

Reiki

This got me started on the esoteric stuff my grandmother just passed away my mother's mother that is Jacqueline and she died of manaesthetic ovarian cancer meaning it was a a a cancer that spread all over the fucking body and he died miserably and I didn't exactly enjoy that experience and having to go to a funeral seeing my see you next Tuesday aunt and other stuff. I was an emotional wreck and then I decided I was through a worker then I met her name is Leah she was very good to me and she taught me About different crystals in how to heal yourself emotionally and physically with different healing stones.   The first thing I made with her was a Chakra bracelet. And then a little charmers Goldstone in it cold Stone supposed to bring you good dreams dreams come true and happiness. And that was supposed to be and then the chakra bracelet supposed to align your chakras I suppose. I want to learn more about Reiki and the esoteric stuff because he was going to help me with my PTSD soon enough I learned about Taro cards, oracle cards, The different crystals and then soon enough I learn more about my past lies I even rat a past life blog called past life Palo Bock I put it on her anonymous cause I was a little embarrassed about that particular past life it was a turd sure and a past life that I had where I was a Buddhist monks lover in Tibet. So I was not very proud past life but I tried to embrace it anyway there were some funny stories with this Leah girl she was she had this friend who is a psychic I didn't know he was a psychic anyway I picked up a crystal that had something to do with PTSD that to heal PTSD it was my car Mika is supposed to be good for helping with PTSD anyways I handed the guy the stone the Mika and I found out from him that I had fairy energy yes fairy energy if you like nerdy things like theory like fantasy horror sci-fi whatever and video games and stuff you're most likely going to be having fairy energy or fairy DNA fairy DNA is not usually discovered on ancestry.ca or ancestry.com so you're kind of fucked on that you can only be detected by a psychic so he ended up giving me a book on fairies for free and I was shocked. Not in a bad way but in a good way and I learned about the different types of fairies and how to encourage a fairy person and my parents were not very good at encouraging me they always told me I talked silly and that I had too much of an imagination. Until one day I came back with some Mika stone in the book and I said I got a fairy energy. Any in this book I remember reading about that Norway do you get fairy energy but you also have fairy DNA which is the kind of form of fairy energy because it this kind of DNA is not detectible on traditional DNA test do you have to go to a psychic to find out about fairy energy and fairy DNA. This has no porn against the

LGBTQ community as I am lesbian but I do have the mystical energy of a fairy and I had I have a very caring heart for people very nerdy and I care about the environment to an extent and another funny fucker of a story was when I was with Leah, was that I was going hiking and this is after I found out I had fairy energy and fairy DNA after I read the book on fairies and then I realized that I was also the proud owner of $180 worth of smoky quartz crystal so we went to Westport to go find out how much this sucker cost it was a big chunk of smoky quartz shamanic smoky quartz and we ended up finding out it was $180 worth of smoky quartz. I ended up leaving that in my room above my bed so I can have shamanic abilities. The Shominique abilities were the abilities to find my past lives and soon enough lucid dreaming which I mentioned in the last chapter. As well as I'm learning different things I was very weird I enjoyed having the crystal the $180 worth of smoky quartz with me until the fucking flood happened. Then it disappeared because some greedy bastard from Canada restoration services took it as well as my mothers old balls and the rest of my healing crystals and I was not tickled when I tried to ask my auntie one time where is my crystals and she said they stole them and I was like what the fuck. So I was not happy. That was why she was my aunt anyway she was kind of a bitch but anyway she turned out to be a bitch. I ended up deciding I was going to move on and car to find other means with crystals to help myself heal and I got myself a Reiki pyramid or Oregonite pyramid, which is a functional piece of artwork you go around with it in your pocket and you expect good luck and then when you meditate or when you're learning something new you acknowledge the pyramid and it likes it and it gives you good luck and helps you calm down it's very interesting. I read up on it before I bought the actual organite pyramid or Reiki pyramid whatever you wanna call aunt Crystal pyramid. Why and I got the organic pyramid I ended up finding there is a lot more to it than just a mood enhancing there was other things that helped with my sleep except I drank coffee a lot I still drink coffee that's my vice some twitch one day decided that I was too old for apple juice and a try to give me a Tim Hortons ice cap and that was the end of it and me and my religion in my culture coffee is the one of Islam so every time I have coffee I get a little buzzed what is the weird bar it's the one of his lawn instead of actual alcohol in Islam we drink coffee that's all right. That's why that's my voice and I don't drink hot coffee I drink iced coffee iced Capps iced Frappuccino's are you cappuccinos or whatever else that is caffeinated with the mean originally and I'll go and drink it. That's the only thing that stands between me and a good night sleep is my little addiction or Weiss which is coffee. But that's a cultural thing not because someone said that I was too old for Apple juice but I realized in a movie there an in box that Muslims typically drink coffee traditionally I don't know there's some them I drink tea but that stuff is caffeinated too so let's just face it is what it is it's the drink beverage of choice for Muslims caffeine. And I am when it comes to caffeine I am a big mouth and a big heart. I just will not shut the hell up and I will not stop being decent I was very strange the coffee it's a very makes me hyper in other words.

Why Sufi

You wondering my name is Sophie why. Because in the Sufism or Sufi Islam we believe that we connect through knowledge to get to God and to the universe as well through knowledge and other rituals like dancing and art and body art. That's where I am such a tattoo thing. And I like my coffee as well as I am a little eccentric and I like to learn as much as I can. I didn't know this was gonna leave me down the road where I'm going to have a career one day. And possibly a social worker or mental health worker I don't know but something big is going to happen. When I finished my first course Christopher said well it's gonna open YouTube one bunch of opportunities I didn't think it was going to be opportunities I was just wanting to learn new things but opportunities it is I guess this was my way of saying hello God this is me and this is who I am supposed to be. So basically I got my purpose handed down or handed to me on a SilverPlatter basically.
This is the end of the story of plenty of other memories and others good things but anyway this is what I think the things happen for a reason that there are connect the dots in life that it's not just random shit or luck or karma that it's just a connect the dot kind of thing like fate. Things happen for a reason in life you might not like them but you'll like the end result in the end if you let it happen. In this case I was abused as a baby by extremist and left for dead by my idiot birthmother then I was put in the Catholic school where my human rights were violated and then I also were given the chance to go A wonderful place where I was able to spread my wings creativity wise and otherwise unable to grow as a human being do I still have to pop the kitty bubble as my brother said yes I do in someways someways I don't have to break the kitty bubble especially if I'm going to be a social worker I need the kitty bubble in order to interact with children and I may have to stop swearing and be sorry swearing is not very becoming of me it's not very good I'm trying not to swear. Because it's not feminine even though now I consider myself non-binary lesbian still I consider myself it's not really of any gender to swear so class wise I mean. I am more of the classy bad ass sassy club girl not the trashy swearing bitch even though I just said bitch. I try not to swear even in my rap music I try not to swear now even though the first album had a lot of F bombs and see words it was a lot of that going on but the second album did not have a single swear word. And I'd rather keep it that way that the swelling stops. And now that I might be a mental health worker or social worker and I have to deal with children I might not wanna swear. So I ended up I might have to tell my brother I might not have to destroy the kid bubble yeah after that I might actually need to use it for a job Monday to get on the kids level so they can help themselves one day so I'm not gonna break the kiddy bubble let's put it that way.
I had a feeling I was going to end up in social work or mental health,why:
The last time I was with my brother was in April and I watched the Papillo which was the new remake of the Papillon which was about the French Guyana prisons and how the people were suffering from psychosis and stuff and I remember what psychosis was caused by and psych class in high school and I learned a lot and I decided I was going to delve deeper - and I was going to find a Squirrley problem my day to learn about and it was very interesting the mind is no different from the night sky except it's inside your head there's a lot of interest intricacies and interesting stuff going on in your head as well as on the night sky as well the night sky just your mind projected but I find that when you look at the night sky your mind is just a pebble or a grain of sand compared to the great vastness of the universe so I just find out my problems even my PTSD are smaller than shit when it comes to the night sky and the universe that's my stepping into the ocean of the universe and that compared to me just a drop of water that ocean of the universe so but the The psychology and stuff and learning about French Guyana and the psychosis that the prisoners went through and stuff in Pappy was very interesting and I love that movie very much because it was very educational I learned about history I learned about psychology I read up on I decide to learn more about the stuff and

that's why my brain guys taste of knowledge since 2013. Sensei and I sensei bro I've been wanting to learn more about stuff in general and that's where I am now thanks to the Papillon movie that my brother had.
Because of certain movies I want I learned certain things that help might help society and also enlighten me in different ways like I learned about that you shouldn't put someone on with PTSD on death row when I was watching emergency and I was also learning about the death penalty process during just Mercy the movie which was very good it's one of my favourite movies as well I also learn a lot of things even from Bollywood films are even like learning different languages and learning stuff there's a reason why I like learning and curiosity doesn't always kill the cat it's because I know what kind of information to look for how to find it and that there is other ways there is a certain type of Internet called the library and the bookstore you should try that one time. Instead of just using an e-book or using the Internet to find out about stuff car to go to a movie theatre library or bookstore you might find something that you might want to do for a living. That's what I think they turn on and watch the Internet it begins with the Internet and it ends with the library movie theatre movie or bookstore but you have to go old-school like library's and stuff before because you cannot rely on the Internet all the time that's what I think and I will tell you something about the Internet that pisses me off that got me interested in doing tattoo art.

Crap and oddities

I think this was in February or January when the Internet went out and I went bat shit. The first time I was able to handle it by doing tons of Creepypasta artwork I believe in creepypasta I love creepypasta and why do I believe in it I'll tell you in a minute but anyway I was doing artwork just to keep myself from going out for the other people in the group home which I don't want to do. So I just shut up and made different types of siren heads like lampshade head lamp had an egg etc. and then I ended up going to self portraits one was prophetic very prophetic over pink hair girl when I realized I was getting a pink hair and wig I was going to think a while that's where I just need the lampshade to go along with it. It was one of my proudest pieces of artwork and I've made some more what you do is you make a crappy template and then you fill in and do the other details later actually it's pretty fun and I do that with my tattoo art as well. I am very honest with my artwork as well and I did a lot of siren head like creatures. I ended up deciding that I was going to try to make T-shirts out of them but couldn't do that anyway I showed them to my brother one time and he thought they were good to the cats miaow especially the girl with the pink hair in the lampshade over her head. When I decided I was finished with art and the Internet was no longer going to continue to go back on I went completely bat shit and went crazy one of the workers Helen at the store and she was going to get me to stay at the bosses house so I can stay certain and not go off on the other people go off meaning throw a temper tantrum natural temper tantrum not a flashback. So I spent the weekend doing artwork and getting to know a guy named I can't remember his name Jack Polock I think he was a very interesting fella we ended up having a bit of a relationship but he ended up blocking me for some funds that reason after the Internet was back on anyway he believed in the same things that I did with the creepypasta in the aliens and siren head and other shit that normal people would find crazy. When I realize he sent me a picture of some UFOs and they were not nocturnal or anything they were exact all photos I realize that this is that there are other people like me out there. Anyway it still sucks to have to be at the bosses house and have to not have the Internet at my original group home it was a pain in the hours one so I was able to get there Internet back I was able to go back and that's when the idiot decided he was going to block me oh that's on him. But anyway this is going to get strange here. And I mean it's going to get really strange there's a couple of incidents in my life where I've come across some fifth kind and I'm not joking this is the actual truth. I remember one time I was playing in the this is number one playing in the schoolyard at grade 7 in lunchtime recess and I supposedly disappeared for most of the recess time and just came back during class and I was in the nude and I was supposedly said anything and I didn't know what was going on. That's when I read later on recognize and I was abducted by aliens why else would I show up in the noodles. In the middle of the day one at the time there was no paedophiles to be around to hurt you so I was able to locate my clothing and stuff for the next recess and I had a towel around me for most of the time I was kind of pissed off that I was born and then in grade 8 exactly to the year and I was 14 at the time my father kept yeah I'm and I thought he was just yelling to be annoying and I told many times to shut the fuck up I know that nice to say to your father but he kind of was a jack ass in the end and then I thought I was just being a jack ass until you said come on and see what I'm looking at and then I saw at three UFOs he said I think they're balloons but I said I don't think they're balloons I know what the hell they are. And I knew what they were they were UFOs why else would he be squawking like a pigeon being washed because he saw something that was not usual. So I saw her you are full and I was adopted by aliens that something that's a little strange. I know you're going to think I'm a fucktard and I'm not but this is basically these are my life a Vance. Anyway I want one day when I was during Covid and I was in the group home here is this story. I got shitty news that my father had two strokes and wasn't going to make it so one of the girls took me out for an ice cap this is the beginning of my addiction that coffee and then I realized she asked me to look at a pond the pond was nice I look but I was more interested in the trees to me like any religion the tree is the sacred part of the universe anyway and then I looked above the trees and I saw some thing that was really fucked up and weird two opposing sirens on a pole. Try to explain that one to me and not say the words Sirenhead OK I'm raising my eyebrows. I actually saw Fuckin Sirenhead and I did not bring my fucking phone with me to take the damn picture and I was madder than a hornet at myself just as mad as I was when I busted the actual razor a few days ago and I was not very happy about that either but this I was mad because I did not have any proof that I saw Sirenhead except for a goddamn witness and I always always drive by that area and see this Is where siren head would be and I would like that's where I saw him that's where I saw him I had asked claim every time I go near my hometown of Almont it was very weird. But yes every time I go near Almaro Carleton Place and I see that pond that exact pond and then I go and see the exact reason I say that's what I saw the fucking siren head. And then I tell a story about how I forgot the phone and I was an idiot not to take a picture. A year later after I heard Mary creepy and melodic silence sounds that were mysterious when I was having dinner outside on the porch last summer a year to the day when I saw the first siren head my father had his two strokes at the same time I know that day was unbelievable but this was crazy I heard the sirens I thought maybe it was the goddamn paramedics next-door but I don't wanna drink them I would recognize I can recognize different shrill noises and different pitches and stuff because I have the ears of a bad that's why I want my spirit animals is the bat. But anyway I ended up finding out this was no ordinary siren from a police or fire or ambulance this was creepy sounding sirens. And I said he must be next door or around the corner that siren head must be in the forest somewhere trying to get his meal to ironically I was having my dinner at the same time that was so I saw siren head and heard siren head on two different occasions. That is about the wacky as it gets with me nobody will ever believe me on these but it's the truth I remember going in that day and I saw the workouts and they were saying listen did you hear that sirens and I said yes I know what it is probably. So I was not very unusual Sirenhead usually hangs around during pandemics in war Time and he usually hangs out in rural to suburban areas..... very rarely has he been seeing in a big city downtown Ottawa like settings so there you go if you see siren head in the downtown city you're crazy but if you see him in the countryside or in your small neighbourhood you're not crazy. In fact this is why this is so Ironhead was popularized by a famous horror artist named Trevor Henderson one of my heroes artistic heroes that is and what it was always around since world war 11 ShellShock or PTSD was around and every time someone went to war and got PTSD or a.k.a. ShellShock they would tell of this creature wins a pole for a head and two sirens on opposing sides of the pole and the creature would be emaciated looking and it would be 48 feet tall now roughly the size of your telephone pole if not more and enemy a source of siren head before Trevor Henderson came around was always spread by people with PTSD oh I saw siren head in Bosnia I saw Sirenhead and Chechnya I saw Sirenhead he are there in this world whatever I want and she will be someone with PTSD that has seen siren head. If you see someone with PTSD who doesn't know what siren head is you got a tasty twirl of which means a poser.   And that's about as wealthy as it gets with me as far as what I've been through I don't usually tell this batch of my life or death say Sufi you're crazy you're not you're insane why do you think this side and a lot of people are very judge mental and I will go around saying all the fucking mental illness that I actually have his PTSD other than that I'm as soon as a bird oh and here's a bird for you ~ middle finger.

The tower: memory

When I was a young girl I used to like to look at my father's magazines whether they be G rated or otherwise I always looked at his magazines. I know I looked at

his a smudy stuff a couple of times and I didn't really like that too much I was like what the hell is there is there anyway soon I got rid of the smut and I ended up looking at his National Geographic and I should are in Vernon Lee learning about my ancestors the first time was the mother Mongolians and I was in ninth grade and I was learning about the Mongolians in National Geographic that's one smut was taken out of the house. Then it was a different Stansly Kazakhstan Uzbekistan stuff and then there is the Uighurs that I pricked my interest as well.
One magazine which was the National Geographic 2005 January or February edition about the Han dynasty that really got my brains juices flowing. This is why I I wanted to find out more about my ancestry list of those magazines but anyway Honda honesty and I read about Xinjiang China in it and that There was this beacon tower /watch tower that was directions to Han dynasty it had a very esoteric and very surreal lock to watch some people and say it looks like a piece of mail and out of me but it didn't look like that to me it looks like a art piece that yeah our nature made. Instead I kept staring at it until I ended up drying out on time in the 1230 when I started drawing it I ended up for screwing up a couple of times and then ended up actually getting to memorize every nook and cranny of this particular beacon tower. It was the kuqa beacon tower, or Karakigil Beacon towers in Kuqa (Kutcha) show me John China it's very interesting to see I always am very interested in looking at it it was part of the great wall at one point but was used as a fire be contour fire water tower. OK watch out for people that have no and good intentions for China at the time I don't really like China now but I do like his people and his culture and that particular Beacon tower here is where the Uighurs live and that's where I'm starting to learn more about my ancestors inadvertently meaning by accident. Before I ended up doing a DNA test I ended up crashing my heritage down from two places the Uighurs and the Tibetans. And the other places in between Bucharest and Peking China so therefore it was very interesting to see that I was Mongolian that's why again the other day I wrecked my darn razor and was not happy about it but that's beside the point I have to stop harping on that anyway I will keep reading up on these places along the silk road in a long there's the northern silk road where the tower is in there is a southern silk road and then yes where Kabul Afghanistan is branches is the spice Road which is very interesting to India. The only kind of spices I can handle are the Indian spices I cannot handle Latin spices they burn my tongue to hell so I cannot have any spicy Latin food instead I can have suicide wings if I pace myself, Or hot wings if I pace myself as the only meat all he is particularly chicken wings and chicken fried rice some beef burgers and a lot of fish I don't really very much of the barny yard but anyway yes I am was able to go through the silk roads and the spice Road and notice where my ancestors were coming from everywhere I see more is coming and then I was like that's why I look a certain way this is why I act a certain way while I have flesh expanders in my ears. Instruction why I'm such a strong person and also why I am so flexible. So I ended up warning that's why I decided I was going to go for the DNA Tash few years later after that when I found out I had some Arab been me one test it was a facial composition test in certain there is Asian black and Arab as well as white. It was the black part that got me pregnant for the DNA test and want me to send in my spirit. I did another DNA test an actual other DNA test called my ancestry or my true ancestry and found out that I have Nubian in me as well that's why I like piercings other than the Asian part of me. I don't want to stereotype but I guess that's why I like rap music sometimes the Nubian. I don't wanna stereotype but that's what it is basically is there a instinctively like hip-hop and rap as well as This. So I was even more of a rainbow than I even expecting to me I was more or less wizard of oz on feet. The only thing I am missing in my DNA map and I don't really need our African-American which I already have the African part the Latino or Native American but I am close to Native American I am Siberian eastern Siberian next to the land bridge I was there decision away from being a full Canadian from being full Canadian. As an indigenous and having a free education and a good culture here instead of having a con Carney of different cultures. That said I guess why I was interested in the different indigenous cultures of North America because I was also very close to

being indigenous I was just a decision away except that one ancestor decided to go west to Europe instead of east to Canada. So that was just a very interesting titbit but the tower I swear to God that tower that I keep seeing in and I always look it up when I want to look at it is very beautiful in Xinjiang and I wonder if it's still around if it is I would go and see it in a heartbeat. There's a couple of places in Asia I wanna go that might not pertain to my DNA like Cambodia I can that's not in my DNA but I will go to Cambodian to see you what is it called island Angkor Wat that was one that I want to see and Japan in Korea and some of China that I'm not related to but I would obviously see this Beacon Tower in the Sinkiang that I've been meaning to see since the 10th grade. If there is something about bareness of the Taklamakan desert and the beauty of the tower in the surreal Nazareth and the lighting of it that really got through to me that I had to see this tower. That I love having past life flashbacks from these guessing the tower every time I looked at that particular magazine. It's very interesting word a picture can do and it can cause a reaction in so many ways that it'll cause you to have passed away flashbacks not PTSD flashbacks past life thousand reincarnational rebirth. The Hindus call reincarnation the Buddhist call it rebirth. That's why I'm so interested in these different religions because I finally find I take something from the hand something from the Buddhist or something from the Muslims and I borrow from them to help me with my PTSD and help me with my problems and I become a mystic in a way........ I guess that's why I took to Reiki and the New Age stuff to duck to water.

Cuba: memory

When I was a kid I used to be more or les Raised at the airport why because my parents like to travel they used to travel a lot before I came along and they travel a lot bringing me along with them. The places I've been to Morocco Cuba the Caribbean show Central in North America and also Hawaii Europe western and Turkey and Greece as well as Heathrow airport I've been around plenty places around this little nerd called earth I call later nerd because of when you say ball it's kind of inappropriate so I said nerd. Or sphere. So I ended up learning a lot about other cultures that weren't really pertaining to my own call service but we're very interesting nonetheless I wanted to learn Spanish when I was a kid why because I went to Cuba a lot as a kid and I always loved Cuba for a swimming pools. I don't care what the country's government was like dresses long as there is a swimming pool again the trouble Wes meeting I can Swimmin. And I will splash like a son of a bitch. But then there was one time when I was almost the end of the trip at Cuba and I threw a hissy fit not on flashback or anything just a plain old hissy fit saying I didn't wanna leave. So I ended up screaming and yelling in front of everyone in the dining room at my parents and I'm not going back to Flippin school that should've been a warning sign to my parents that Catholic school was not for me but anyway they just say well they know what makes me feel happy other than H2O at the time which was stargazing so the wind took me to the beach at night we went walking around the beach at night it was a clear ass night I saw the big difference

in a little different I said very randomly that's the big dipper which wasn't a random little dipper not a random that must be north not too random as well and then I said that must be Miami Florida that scared my father. As he checked the map that was near our hotel the other day after that he ended up being a frayed of my intelligence not in a bad way but I know I don't know what kind of person I raised or created kind of way like I'm surprised kind of way. So I always wanted to be an airline pilot when I after that time because why I'd be looking at the big dipper encompasses another thing I know what half an hour cardinal direction is north south east west the usual. And I would go in the middle of winter after I got back from Cuba and sit on the swing set and just look at the stars I wouldn't see the Pletit I didn't know what the ple I just called the little big dipper and then I would go and see the big dipper and the little Debrah I well that's north and I always pointed out randomly that that was north as if I had a compass inside me. It was strange the abilities that I learn when I travel it was kind of odd and then I freaked my father out again the same way in Miami and I said that is Orion that mean must be south and where Cuba is I was about 121 years old at the time and he was freaked out again Danny check the map again said damn it she's right.
That was the time one I just started I was gonna have my IQ tested just for the hell of it to see what it's gonna be I knew it wasn't going to be anywhere near Chamonix it would be close to the 130 so I knew that but when I did not know is that I did not get the genius IQ level I got the superior level which is it 180+ to be more exact my IQ is 196 again I mentioned this before and some people would say that I'm crazy to say that but I do have there so I Carol I had it tested by Mansa and it was just to see and for a laugh and then it turned out it wasn't a laugh it was serious that I had this IQ that was through the roof. That's why I can read a book faster than anyone and enjoy it at the same time my parents always sad " What was slow now on the reading got to thick book why don't you pay attention it and I said yes "I did pay attention to the book tell you a fun fact about it blah blah blah blah blah blah."
What got me reading books in the first place so it's not because of school or a curriculum but because I had enough of my father's bad taste in movies he like crime dramas and film the water or something I didn't like the real slow movies I like a fast pace Chinese drama he like his stupid FBI thrillers which were pretty stupid at the time and there was one it was so slow and I was lucky enough there was a book in front of me so I picked up the book and that's what ended it from there and I never looked at the TV said again except for Netflix no 15 years later when I was 33 years old that I never really even out there it's lucky enough to get in a glance because of my courses that I'm taking I am very reading like and I like to read and do a lot of writing. Is weird how are you gonna learn about yourself from one book and the world from another book but that's what it is that's why they're there they're the Internet of the old and there's still quite viable and valid.
I started writing poetry before WordPad and then I ended up writing poetry on Twitter one of the people that I used to work with that worked with me actually said she had a friend who is an author and I had a book signed by that woman gala green. And she said good luck with the Writing in a in the book and then obviously here I am now today.   I am a 3 times yummy reads author. I have 3 different pen names. Lily Lisa bubbles, and I have a word account for each one of them so I can close them on my rocky Kindle direct publishing account. It's very hard how the imagination can go so far when you can't stand a movie. That you would end up reading a book and then the next thing you know your three time yummy reeds author.

Halloween

Halloween has always been my favourite holiday because of why I don't have to wear my natural hair colour or wear anything that I don't wanna wear it's a time when I can be who I am without being told off. Meaning bullied sometimes I always enjoyed going trick-or-treating dressed and get dressed up and to go out. I would dress up usually as an alien because I was fascinated with aliens as a kid I would be interested in outer space and stuff so I had a green face sparkly face and a green wig and incana as well as a garbage bag over my rollers. It was very fun to go trick-or-treating I never grew out of it. So in my taste in costumes change from alien the pharaohs to the samurai and then to now yakuza.   Just recently I have discovered special effects make up when I was going as a dead bride it was very interesting so I decided to learn more about it myself that was the E before last year. I ended up learning how to do the make up myself and then I ended up becoming a meet up yeah Cusa for Halloween as trick-or-treating costume yes it was very fun I had a pixie cut sunglasses and my boss now. And I would always grade them with the Yakuza greeting I know a thing or two about that. From box. So I was fine when I was trick-or-treating and I knew all the poses and stuff From the way of the house husband which is the Netflix series that I sometimes watch is an anime series it's pretty interesting the guys pretty loud and annoying but he's pretty funny. Tatso is his name.

That was not an easy month for me that month of October as I had problems with my aunt on Thanksgiving Canadian Thanksgiving to be exact. Supposedly she invited my mother but didn't invite me which was a real see you next Tuesday move. And I called her on it and told him I'll call my mental health worker on her and tell her that she's a see you next Tuesday and she was being really when she about it let's put it that way so she a harassing me and then playing mind games and stuff like that and then one time recently when I was with my brother I found out she was saying that I was a psychopath and that I was the game player but really it wasn't true and I said that is a pile of crap and I told my mother she better get rid of that sister of hers because her sister was going to be nothing more than Croatian she is of the psychopath she is the manipulator in the game player not me because I am an honest human being I have emotions empathy and everything else I don't have a single warning sign for psychopathy where is my hand on the other hand is a complete animal. And I said I know a thing or two about mental health to my mother I know a thing or two about water what it what it takes to be a psychopath and it means no emotion no remorse no empathy not giving a damn and that was my aunt in a nutshell I was hopping mad and I was crying that day and my brother was beside him self because he didn't want me to tell my mother about this but I had to tell her she had a right to know that her sister was a see you next Tuesday. I might have my problems but I am not like Oren Ishii from kill bill or anyone by that matters of that Ted Bundy or anything so why did she have to say that stuff was gone off all my and why is that was. He says it takes one to no one usually and if you say someone is a psychopath it usually means you make the best psychopath to it just a saying but it's true.

She was always causing problems for me and I had a call the lady of the house many times that weekend to say listen I need to strong any order against my aunt for her safety because she's going get in trouble with my hands and stuff because she called me these names. And that she was the one causing the mind games and stuff since October it was not very easy for me and they were just horrible it was just a horrible time that's why I decided to block her on Facebook and I said to my mom I'm blocking my ass off Facebook and I'm just phoning her and I'm also disowning everyone else in my mothers family except for my mother my mother was the lucky dog she didn't get this song. Another see you next Tuesday move that my aunt did was hiding my citizenship card when I needed to renew it we never found it ever again she hit it real good and I never's and I was madder than a hornet because she was this was one of her games again. I remember her crying to one of the workers and saying this is what's going on and I'm mad and I'm afraid for my safety and stuff that I might be kicked out of the country in Software actually I was reassured that that was the opposite except for the aunt playing the games the aunt was a pissant I thought. Will I tell you the name of this particular family member former family member and I will not because she will just go back crap on me right away and start playing her games again I wouldn't be too surprised if she was holding my mother's old bowl as well as my healing crystals as well as any house just to get through to me. It was a very awful so I think about but she was a horrible human being and start in October 2021 and it continues to this day I had to switch Netflix accounts from the bitches account to my group homes account just to prove a point that I don't need her anymore. She was a very horrible person and I still believe that she is still playing games with people I know one of her sons does anti-VAX her what is not very good.   And at the time of the Thanksgiving dinner I accused my mother of adopting one of my cousins because I was having a flashback I was a very horrible time. I still have a hard time getting over that and it's a sore spot to think about.

Kindness

They are having some random stuff in my library is random as of the word kindness why do I say that because I would go and I see something I would want and someone will give it to me for free and they said just pay it back to the client yes and that is for her what I've been told many times. Is there an usual but it does happen from time to time someone pays for your coffee and you don't have to pay when you pay it forward with cleaners or another act of kindness as well or kind access kind of random but as nice as well and it's means good locations on my calls or just do that to be kind of someone and then the next thing you know you got good luck back from being kind. I am a very big fan of paying it forward if I can.
As a kid and I many times has a younger adults one guy was either on Cruise vacation on a bookstore and they say here you go this you might like you can have it Isaiah I don't have the money and I'll just keep it anyway. Because I would be a very loyal customer or I need loyal person to them or or there was just being nice and knowing that I don't have the amount of money that I would usually need it's not it's just trying to help someone out and says no different if you're in line

for coffee and someone else's I'll pay for the person behind me that's why I was more last since it's really random one these things happened. It's like excuse me I and even if I do have the money they sometimes say just take it it's yours and I am like OK thank you. But I also would give them the money I have in my pocket just to be nice to them and it would be honest to give them as much as I could for whatever they're giving me but they were to refuse the money at some points sometimes they would take the money and say OK I'll take that amount. It's very interesting how kindness can go around or how flexible people can be when I want to be where are you on your decent human being and you have a infectious personality somebody like me for example you trying to go and attract the kindness of others and you bring it back forward to other people as well like one person gave me a uncle John's bathroom reader out of the blue knowing that I wanted it but I didn't know that at first she said you I know you don't have the money and she gave it to me anyway I left with a free book and was weird. So I said I'm gonna have to pay it forward somehow so I made a painting for someone else and gave them that painting and then it was a snowball in the wrong kind of kindness it's not that hard to be kind is very simple to be flexible or kind and see the smile on somebody's face if you say yes go ahead have it like for example I was at a ball game the other day I could've easily's nest in the mall that nearly flew in my face but instead I let the little girl have the mall because I thought she would appreciate it more than I would I would just get a piece of paper and get my autographs after the game and be happy with the autographs I still have to frame the autographs as far as the mall was concerned the stray ball what is the little girls because I wasn't going to snag some thing that was just going to leave dust on my dresser.

This is my first ball game I want to and I want and I actually enjoyed it it was the Iowa Titans and I enjoyed my time there they had so many different kinds of music I was very entertaining you wouldn't expect this with a ball game but it was very good baseball is one of my favourite sports now you're not because of the autographs or nearly getting hit in the face with the baseball but but because I actually enjoyed seeing the game and I enjoyed getting my second pair of autographs in one week I'll tell you I've had another set a pair of autographs from country Hall of Famer like a country music Hall of Famer and his wife who are the band team and I ended up getting both other autographs and I ended up finding out that they also said good luck in their autograph and I said that's right that's weird that says if they know I'm a musician too that was good I was very happy about that I want it that was at a talent show where I'm going to go to play the steel Toungedrum next month or the month after that I don't know when I'll tell you more about the steel Toungedrum is A dome like round drum that you had certain cut areas semi-cut areas to make certain sounds with and it's very interesting it came from Asia particularly China and to Beth and as many as way to east Turkistan and then to the way of the west usually hippies usually play but I like to play it because it's calming for my PTSD as well as it's fun and easy to play I can easily make songs of it and stuff and I actually was hosting a ladies night at my apartment and I actually brought out the steel Toungedrum and everyone enjoyed the steel tongue drum the sound that was and I just continued playing it as if to entertain that was my first time next time will be the concert I'll have to mention that one time in another work but I am moving up in the world I think. Because well I want to see you a little deal tongue drum and the other because people are kind to me they give me free courses are they saying even have this if you want if you don't have the money or you give me what you got or something like that is very important to be kind.

I remember reading and chicken soup for the teenage saw that a girl saw guy having a rough time and she gave him a nickel or a dime I don't know some kind of coin that had a monetary value and it helped him through his rough time and he's thanks a girl and then he actually didn't have to do anything to hurt himself and he actually went on with his life and he thanked the girl for that I was very inspired by that particular story it's very weird that one random even a small thing can go as far as whether be a coin or an autograph can go so far. That's why I suggest that you give back to the world if you can in small amounts and then see what you can do in big amounts like careers and then go from there that's why I decide hi want to help people with life whether be giving them a random Christmas present even though they say no no no give me a Christmas present I'll still give them the darn Christmas present or I do something with my life that's productive or something it's very important to give back as I said I remember my mom blasting my radio drum because I walked all the way to my friends house and back and she thought I was just going to my other friends which was weird. But it inspired me to think. Think about it if you do something Good it doesn't have to be like being an FBI agent or a police officer it just means giving someone something small and that they'll take a mile from edge and they'll take a mile from it in a good way. That's what I think and I found one I was given the courses last night for the first time did my first course that that was my mile my end that made a mile in my life and in my day. The guy said there wasn't nothing much it was just that he also does a free online courses so he can have a good career too but I was very Particularly interested in the world around me and now I might have something going for me and I might be giving back in kindness as well.

Cobra Kai

When I start watching Netflix one of the favourite shows I liked was cobra Kai no because it was a mount martial arts but I was about how marsh war should be a form of meditation and mindfulness. That mindfulness is just as simplest taking that deep breath and we're walking away and distracting one sell through martial arts or whatever you do that is fun. It doesn't have to be so theoretical like DBT or CBT. In fact it's just a deep breath may be a few crystals here and there and a little bit of happiness and kindness once a day will help you out. I found that with cobra Kai especially talks about how anger is either good or bad depending on how you choose to use it but then again I can say the same thing about the Insane Clown Posse which my mother hated with a passion was insane clown posse and she didn't understand it until I said well the lyrics do sound a little off caller what they're saying is that make a productive life make me a good person to be yourself/ be who you are in the first place and use your anger to create instead of hate. This is the same thing with cobra car except it's a TV show and there's no clowns involved. There are mark two waring dojos cobra car and Miyagio Miya o do you teach us more about mindfulness and trying to shape your future and stuff which I found very interesting and I wanted to get a bonsai tree just for the sake of mindfulness. And then there's cobra Kai which is just a pain in the butt where they teach anger and bullying. I know I sound like a child they're saying bullying but that's what they were still are in the show because the show is still continuing I always watch that show religiously because I enjoy it and it's fun to watch. My favourite is Hawk when he turned from negative anger to using it into a positive and helping them Yanni dolls. He was very good and he was a Barnery brother of Dimitri I don't know what his last name was but anyway it was very good show Steelers and I'll be waiting on September to watch it. This is the only thing that I watch on Netflix other than a few social issue shows I don't really want very much TV except for Netflix or Tubi or YouTube and that is just to entertain myself other than that I read like a fiend. I know I should be doing my DBT stuff for my PTSD but the DVD is just a way of saying I am complicated whereas if you go and learn about mindfulness as it supposed to be which is taking a deep breath taking some time alone instead of the lot easier on you than having to learn the SDS acronym on that acronym so I watch Netflix for that instead like a cobra Kai instead and I am very glad hey Siri of mindfulness has been brought to my attention with this amusing TV show that has been created by the karate kid franchise I'm very proud of that show and I am proud to say it's my favourite show. It's very important to have this kind of show on TV shows it's important to be polite nice and mindful and that you have to be mindful of what you do with your anger and how to handle it. There's one guy in cobra Kai on online John Kreese who I call Casey twirl and we've all heard tasty total weight for a PTSD poser someone pretending to have PTSD I don't know how anyone can do that but it's very easy it's just hang out I had a flashback or there's any other thing I need to actually have the actual flashback and acting like a more or less an animal and using those for ladders as an excuse. Some thing I cannot stand in fact I am actually thinking if I ever go on some serious serious money I'm climbing Mount Everest and this is not a joke to say that people were PTSD are not the devil or the flu we are just people that have bigger emotions and bigger nightmares and bigger anger sometimes that's it. And we're only human and I am gone that's one thing I've been telling my mother I'm gonna climb mount Everest for PTSD awareness and acceptance we've already heard about autism awareness and acceptance but no one really likes PTSD for some odd reason because of the Simpsons stuff the Simpsons have really stigmatized people with mental illness like PTSD and it drives me nuts. To the point where I'd like to get the guy who created the show and say hey listen you can't stigmatize people over a certain disease or Mental illness you can't make fun of them because of that they're not all serial killers or strangler some of us are human beings are kind of just take a bathroom break kind of thing you know we're trying to deliver lines. So I never really liked the Simpsons amor a family guy saying they're not as stereotyping I find the more hilarious in the Simpsons it will say wow girl with pink hair has listens to punk rock well GuessWhat I listen to old country rap techno punk gothic and industrial.

Give me I think a lot of people like me you have been routed out of school I've rived out of school because of The Simpsons shows like the Simpsons and other horrible things and then end up on the streets and stuff that's what I think and then they end up with the cultures that are not too savoury like a drug addiction violence in criminal activity one really the person with a man a little message just trying to live a life in the school and they get expelled because they have a mental wellness it's really ridiculous and it's because of the Simpsons I it called Simpson shit.   And if you like this show me Susan this is not the book for you because I'm not gonna have this racism and able ism going on where you have to go around being perfect all the time or you're gonna be stigmatized and made fun of. People get home most all the time and they get homeless because they don't get along with their families that's one the other is because there's family drug addiction or alcoholism the other is that they might have a mental illness as well and have no choice but to drop out of school and life in general and go on the streets that's what it is basically what it is. You don't have to make a parity out of it in fact if you do you may as well just route ram yourself right down to the Hades. In other words hell.

That's why I learn my first course I wanna learn if there are also two people that have been stigmatize and have to go in the streets because of their orientation and other stuff that is really again because of the Simpson's I find in popular culture.   Popular or calm and does not mean it has the exactly moral.

When does Kohl's real well drugs or alcohol or sex or treating more everything it's not right here and I'll get to that was my first boyfriend I had and he was a pain in my butt.

I remember my mother saying that I should fit in with the other girls and I said star themselves and go blonde I don't think so be straight and her her her and just being the cookie cutter person no I wanna be who I am,sooooo....... One day I told my mother to go fuck her self for telling me to fit in I wasn't gonna go to parties I was gonna have sex I wasn't gonna be like you other girls will starve them selves or go away go blonde early like everyone else know I was gonna be who Iam and live until 115.

E

Tisha

Ring from grade aid I remember a girl named tisha she was a very nice girl Tisha was a girl who is also a prankster and an old cast in the world of school. She knew that catholic school was not that good for her either. I was agreeing with her that there was too much religious stuff going on in Catholic school and that it wasn't right for everyone. But we were also pranksters as well I was worried I can tell you the many pranks I have pulled with tisha.
Siri head a lot of times together lotta good times Mikasa we have gone play video games on my 16th birthday we have seen them on Narnia he's been through me when I went through my mountaineering phase. But it wasn't really a phase afterwards after I found out I had PTSD and how people with PTSD were treated like Dalits. Something I go inside because assassins Creed with me all day. So I ended up not watching the Simpsons to Unless I wanted I raunchy laugh. Really do I want anything by the Simpsons creator I don't even want this enchantment on turn on Netflix because I just can't stand the concert stereotyping other people it's not right. Anyway one time when I was in grade 11 and I was frightened for my own safety one time on a guy name Matt it up talking to Mary Celine and how are you

doing it's rainy and I ended up what the fuck why is he talking to me I'm the meanest person on the planet at the time and he was talking to me. It wasn't later that he ended up realizing I mean I can get it when I started accusing him of cheating and I had tisha walls as well.   T-shirt made her she would contact me from mad now I still was dating him that was seem like a sweet guy at first but then he ended up talking to a very unusual amount of girls. Something that made me very suspicious and I wanted something done about it she knew about my religion or religions and I ended up deciding to tell her that he's peeing on me what some girl that was of the same races me whenever a race that is mixed. So I ended up telling her she said well then screw a dog. And then after that she when I invite him to the table she said let's have a holy war something I'm really shocked this shit out of me and I nearly slapped her for saying.
How is your arm is the friendship or the beginning of the end of the friendship pretty soon I ended up going back to the school for a grade 12 part one and she ended up saying after and this really made me wanna slap her even more was the fact it's a sad that she wanted to shoot some kid in the head with an AK 47 and I said what the fuck did you say that sure it was just at first day Nas and I said in your heart is the three religions you should be a little bit more respectful and she said I can't he's in a whore and I said I don't care either one you don't have to go around saying that stupid terroristic stuff and she ended up losing a friend over that that day she ended up saying good night instead of alone. And I left. Soon enough to know your self no one very well in my life even though I can't get her out of my life. And then at the end of the first year of grade 12 I had to take grade 12 twice because of the stress level my PTSD. She just made a living hell for me.
Soon one time I was trying to God five times a day and one and the first five times a day I cried so please help me and I said no makes me crying from my God and that's away with it and then I ran up to her the next day and said I want my fucking two year year my life back that your people store. In other words she was a terrorist I was so slightly more thought about that and I had the luck supposedly I have the luck of the devil and I was going hard to the point where he never wants from the corner supposedly for another kid saying Sufi you really got her in a corner.   That's when I realize that destructive anger was a great way to go about things which wasn't really true when I think of it in the long run right now at my age of 33 I was 18 at the time I'm 33 now and I think that was a stupid move on my part trying to intimidate her because she's fat and because I cried while praying I decided I had enough of the anger when I was 23 years old and I started forgiving her.
When I think the real cat was sure was mad because Matt was a real dog to begin with and he was nothing more than a dog and he wasn't that good looking did the get with so let's just say it he was the reason why she went a little woo hoo. So I ended up giving her anything less and less time to be friends again and let's try not to get on each other's nerves it work for a while with your friends on Facebook for three years until I was 30 years old.... Then we parted ways are never talk together. I think Matt must've had a curse on me because I remember my dating life to be nothing more than hell I was trying to be straight one time to talk to Laurie and that didn't work because they were cheating on me and then I try and then I came out as lesbian and that didn't work out either because the girls also cheated on me or they were fake or they were a man in the sky just a girl I didn't like it very much so I decided let's have friends instead instead of dating. And see what happens there.

Wigs

One time I wanna dye my hair bleach my hair talking to my brother randomly he was showing me Different wigs, Then it realized mean instead of having to call about him spending hundreds of dollars a month and have an my head bald time I didn't like a colour so that was pretty good. I'm going on rocky.ca to see if anything was going to show up in the wigs department and I found nine wigs eight of which of the colour of the rainbow and one was the colour I wanted which was gray white. I ended up deciding that's what I was going to do instead of hair dye and bleach because I have tattoos to think about. Something that I've been thinking about lately and the value of money you here don't really care about money but nose please I have so many tattoos designs so many tattoo ideas for my body and I just rather not bother with small stuff if I can help it like stupid hairdydying stupid bleach which would cost me 100 bucks a month and would cut into my tattoo fund. Instead of my hats wins instead of dealing with hair dye and bleach I would wear a hat with the wig but that's little old hard core on my wig so I decided not to hot all the time. I usually wear the wigs instead my favourite colour of the wings is pink and I usually wear the pink most of the time. I am now honest girl with the pink hair sometimes. And that's why it is when I first started wearing a pink wig my favourite colour of the mall I ended up being mistaken as someone else like did we get a new client or something I was like no it's me Sophie and I ended up going around showing that I was in my face is very entertaining at first but then when I went into a store I bought an astronomy book which was good but one processor is not working and I said yes and I pulled it off and showed my true hair colour and I said yes it is a wig because I can't stand my hair color. And I can't stand spending money on stupid chemicals even more I may as well be smoking cigarettes which is another damn story that I'm gonna tell you that is a little obscene and sad. I ended up one time I'll tell you this I took a puff of the cigarette one time then the day when I was getting the actual money for the wigs I ended up huffing huffing puff Lang and I ended up cursing and swearing in front of a little kid holding my knees trying to catch my breath I said this was the end of the cigarettes I wasn't even gonna bother if anyone was worried about me I was worried about me as well I wasn't I knew other people were worried that I was probably awful passing as I Collett now is very derogatory word for people who smoke now Hufflepuff that's what she end up doing is half of puffing in the side of the road morning I got brass and I decided I didn't wanna have that name put on me by myself so I said after this I'm done and I said in front of the kid Canada wearing a new word while she was not too good and I ended up having to say yeah I'm quitting because I've had enough of hufflepuffing.

It was one thing for people to be worried about me one thing but then I decided when I was swearing in front of that little kid I didn't wanna have to have anything to do with the cigarettes anymore it's one thing to have them if you're driving to and from bad and when you're walking forget it even if you're not walking forget it so I decide the hell with this stuff I can find better tasting things at all give me a lot better and I can catch my breath a lot quicker. Trying to get that Rocky card gift card was like climbing Everest that day and I was cursing and swearing every moment. Something that was supposed to be fun turn into something that was embarrassing and that's when I said the lady of the house it I quit smoking I've had it just said the F word in front of a two year old. Something I'm not happy though but it had to be done and I'm glad that I said that I didn't not glad that I said in front of the swearword in front of the kid but it had to be sad because I was in dire straits and when I'm in dire straits I swear. But nurse Casey said this was so embarrassing I bet if the kids mother ran out she would've gave me a talking to and I would've had to say listen I'm kind of catch my breath I have breathing problems but I don't really have breathing problems it was just me being an idiot once upon a time so I decided never mind the cigarettes I called them Hufflepuff's because you're hustling and puffing and ask you was like the big bad wolf where I was trying to blow down a house blow blow blow blow blow it was really embarrassing and I didn't enjoy it one bit. But then it was worth it in the end when I got the wigs all the colours of the rainbow especially gray white it was wonderful and then the day of the wigs coming I went to the library is the same distance as the place that sells sea gift cards and I was able to only have two coughing fits and then I was able to meet a dog named Mickey and I was able to go on with my life and say wow that was a breeze. And it was a breeze breeze going in and out of my mouth and nose instead of a Hufflepuff. If I were to tell you this and I'm gonna tell you this now if you think that smoking is cool or it's in or whatever I'll tell you it's out it's stupid. You're gonna look more like a dork if you take that selfie with a cigarette and you'll be in more people trouble with yourself than you will with anyone else believe me because yourself will cause you more problems than anyone else. And I was hard on myself the day I want to get the gift card but the second time I want to go for the walk it wasn't that bad. But as I said I wouldn't do something stupid to seem cool do you want to be cool just be yourself and be who you are in the first place and don't start anything that's going to start up a coughing fit. Particularly with chemicals it's not right. But that's my opinion on that. Now back to the wigs, when I got back from the library and I found the Panzik trucks they're also trying to give me my Waze I whipped on my Covid mask and was able to go and get the wigs and I was trying each colour on and I liked each colour I found but pink was my favourite to be exact as well I'm a girl you know I say I'm non-binary besides the point of a girl I say she her, and it was a neon pan can I was a very nice colour and I enjoy the colour neon pink very much so I wear most of the time that's why I am the girl with the coloured had all the paint care. I was enjoying myself with the wings and I forgot it was suppertime I think I remember that day and I just put the words away and start reading a book on the Ojibway peoples which was even better, and books that I got from the library.

The people at the library are very nice to me they actually delivered my books when the wigs were coming at the same time I remember they said well are you walking and I said yes as if they knew I took that puff and said let's have you have them deliver to you I'm going up your street anyway so I'll deliver your books for you and I said OK fine thank you again the the randomness of kindness that I enjoyed very much and I got a free the LGBTQ flag a miniature one.   The books I can't wait to read I'm reading one right now which is you one about the a jibway masthology and then I have a bunch of thrillers and I'm gonna read psychological thrillers so I'm gonna learn more about the brain which is good. Something I like Demi Berkshire more addictive than anything else and books and coffee or go together they help make a hyper brain and a very creative brain that's what I think.

Earning my ;

Ring the semicolons on my middle finger juice more than just going to the tattoo parlor. It was in life experience as well as learning about suicide prevention just for interest sake and help other people who might randomly need it. So I ended up learning about suicide prevention can you do something that I was interested in and was very passionate about still am. I said I love her to Paul Ryan get the semicolons without the siding to earn them yard noches with in life experiences it's called but also not without the proper knowledge to make people aware of the subject in the first place. When I was in my early 20s I had a really rough time with my life where I rather not talk about it but I'll tell you anyway where I had a bit of a hissy fit and I threatened myself to my parents and they took her to the hospital and it took more energy and time to cause a kick up of dirt instead of saying while I've screwed up. So I ended up acting like a child and I don't want this value anyone's feelings but that's what it was like for me back then and when I look back on it and I said this was not worth picking up some dirt and wasting time and energy. For something that is so insignificantly and so temporary it's ridiculous I didn't wanna bother with that so I decided fuck it I wasn't gonna bother with that kind of a thought lifestyle anymore. I thought lifestyle was the score of your own thought I decided I was gonna say tough it out ride the wave and then just acknowledge and go ahead with life that's what I decide to go on with then when I decide to do the suicide prevention course so I can make more people more aware of it I need out learning that I was more interested in psychology and mental health and I was with astronomy even though astronomy is one of my favourite things the one thing that I think I was put on this planet for was for to help people and make people aware of mental health that's why I was given these free courses I believe everything happens for a reason I believe and that's why this is why I came around on this planet this sphere. Why I travel the world halfway across the world and why I like learning languages and learning different things in the first place. That was the start and the taste of some thing that now it's going to become something bigger was just trying to earn two silly tattoos that was meaning in life experience but I wanted to make it mean something more than I know about it. The tattoos were not silly just and tell you the truth anything with a semicolon is not silly in fact it means your life should continuo on your story should continue and I believe that's important no read up on even if you're not going to be going down the same fateful path as I am I think we should still learn about the origins of the semicolon and suicide prevention and help with your fellow man it might help someone else as I said give an inch they'll take a mile you never know and that doesn't have to be a bad thing as I said before it can be a good thing they can thrive after you do a simple good thing. Like talking to them in this case. I also learned from that course that you should not diminish or devalue the persons feelings but acknowledge them and say well yes they are what they are and I said I can't think of anything right now but I have been through these doldrums many times as a teenager as well as in my early 20s I don't remember writing a poem and as a little distrubing bird anyways this is what it was, that made my parents say that I was gifted but I had to stay back a year for grade 12. Here is the part of the poem that I remembered anyway it was very easy dark and I wasn't very fun

I'm sorry I was doing computer literacy class
I got in my chair no notice nobody cares I just happened and I naturally
When you realize what happened to me they ended up calling ME
While he was performing my autopsy I begged him not to perform the autopsy instead

I was gonna tell him everything that happened.......... And the polo mostly goes like that most of the time and it was enough to freak out my parents and I flaked me out too and I was only in grade 11 it was there January 2006 I think. And another stressors that year as well I had a religious teacher that was really fascist station say that but she was horrible she wouldn't let you eat lunch unless you were quiet and I was quiet most of the time in that class but I ended up paying for everyone else is bad karma which wasn't Too fun how to tell them about that, my parents and daughter that was so I ended up having to say well and I have this teacher that starving everyone in this class because everyone else is rowdy and I'm the one that has to suffer for it that's why I made me some pounds so I kind a gain weight was some kind of stressor is well for me at the time as well as computer literacy class and the stupid religion class and the teacher that wouldn't let anyone go to lunch it was so stupid.
Well it did get better my first year of gray 12 at least. There is another another person who is going to say or downplay my emotions and downplay me with religion. One girl said the Saddam Hussein should've not been hung and I called her a bitch. That was the girl that my boyfriend Matt was cheating on me with I still remember her name Alex she was a real winner. Anyway it showed up on my Report card and said that I was a zealout But I was not the one saying evil things. I was just trying to state an opinion that someone who was being a pain in the butt and saying that I bad person you should've not had what was coming to him that was really ridiculous on her partner and I was just calling her out on it. She ended up taking my boyfriend away from me that year and I remember that was very horrible and I got into a fight with him and called him an Al-Qaeda sympathizer it was really horrible.
The next day after they have fried I remember dinosaur and I was going to go a different direction as far as my dating was concerned and I told my parents that I was lesbian they excepted me but I didn't know who I was in love with I said I just don't like guys anymore because of Matt because they all cheat and they all lie some of them not all of them there's some good ones out there but there's someone is that a real pains in the toushe.
Set a timer I was banned from my space and I had to wait until Spacey came along to continue my MySpace career which was very annoying because of one piglet that couldn't keep his pants on when I say it was very horrible and I didn't like that one that he should've been the one without the mice face. And guess what he was doing he was calling his mom and saying that I was a criminal and she threaten me with every prisoner on the planet as well which was even worse she said if I even went as far as to go near her son map I was going to be thrown in prison a particular US prison in Cuba that I'm not gonna mention and I was very mad I and I told my mom she was even matter at the mother of this idiot. So that stymied my dating life for the rest of my life ever since then I've had nothing but problems with this guy Matt and I am because of him I've been jinxed so I just go about around talking to people and being friends instead of dating. Which is a better approach than having to date someone and then be jinxed and feeling like you're cursed.

Taking a break

After high school I take a break from education because I was afraid it was gonna be too stressful I didn't know that learning could be fine in the first place until I wish my current age what is 33 years old. What happen when my brother Jonathan taught me about RF which is radio frequency and I ended up winning or passing 100% on that test and course then I ended up winning hundred percent on WiMMS which was not too hard Wi miss was not very hard for me at least it was science. So I ended up and I was always on the lookout for these different certifications and different kind of free online courses that I can take but it was they are very hard to fine. So I ended up going back this is me going back to my present time. I ended up going to Khan Academy on the App Store on the iPad started up with astronomy then I started working my way with calculus scared of calculus but I'm still gonna learn it and the other sciences this is not a bragging rights this is the truth and then I'm also learning about the other stuff that I told you that might get me into a good life and not just financially but emotionally as well I rewarding career as a social worker in which is weird strange to think that would be the route that I would take being someone guiding someone kind of like a big dipper guiding someone through a rough time in helping them like someone trying to golf navigate through C or a forest and go through and find the big dipper and find their way back that's usually what I can see it out and it's not gonna be as simple as the courses bar is going to be pretty interesting and I have to take extra courses for that but I don't mind but when I this is my end of my break from education I decided I had a no wire I stand in the world. And this is not a pile of junk this is the truth Christopher the guy that got me hooked up to the courses had got me to be coming of age I actually learned how to care about other people and not stress care but actually be honestly caring and decent human being and the person that I wanna be you for the rest of my life. It's very easy to take a break from school and find what your true path as I know about the boondoxx song the rapper boom docks in the song I walk the path on the path or something along the line where he says he only wants his own path he's a juggalo which means he is with the Insane Clown Posse. Something that is he also that song about the path was a very good song and it had a good meeting to it as well like any other of the ""psychopathic records what's you're not really psychopathic. They teach you more morals than their school or religion will ever teach you even though it's music and it has a lot of swearing in it. The fact that I listen to that music I found my path through I also found a path in music with steel Toungedrum and wrapping. Hip-hop I mean I talk about my emotions and I tell people white and white not to do like advice through rap that's when I find what route means a case is advising people not to do or want to do in life and not to act a fool and stuff that's when I find a rap music is about so that's why I am passionate about rap music and music so I can keep a good message going. I still play the guitar from time to time though I am taking a break from that right now just get my brain fed with the other courses that I have and then I'm gonna go from there and go back for the guitar after I get the courses done. But I am very excited at the prospect that I am being certified for certain things which is very good and as I'm doing this for want to feed my brain knowledge which is good this is important I would if I had to mentor a kid I would tell them that it's important to find these free online courses and learn as much as you can in life that's what life is about learning and loving life and trying to deal with your emotions in a more positive note. I remember I got a Reiki pyramid and I always carry it around your way to keep the good times rolling in life mean and keep the good energy going and keep the good vibes going it's very interesting how that goes. And I also I'm very kind of people sometimes I don't seem like it but usually I'm kind of people and I am very honest and trustworthy I don't say stupid stuff if someone says I'm not a snitch let's say I don't let out things that aren't meant to be let out that's what I can say. But I do I'm very trustworthy but I'm also honest if I have to be. That's been the way I've been since the day I've been born I've been trustworthy loyal honest and I've been brought up that way and born that way.

I don't know what is palm from morals are at saying that can be passed on by DNA but if it is it's part of the soul at least I think that's what it is and part of my past logs that I've had in my many lives before this particular life came around me. I believe I was a Vedic astronomer in my past life of Vedic mean in Hindu astronomer which means I was your Brahman. I know that sounds funny but it's nicer word meaning hire Rob I believe my class for Hindu priest and four advises an intellectual leaders something I find that I am except for the Hindu priest called I'm not that feeling and I have too much of a party mouse to be a Hindu priest but I am an intellectual and adviser to some people I say OK you shouldn't do this because I've been through this before. So I'm a Brahmin in this life as well if you ward. And I will be continuing to educate and advise people on certain things and I find interesting and then I find passionate about and that I will hopefully lead people down a good path one day and I'm not talking any nonsense my aunt might think I'm an manipulator but really I'm not I'm just trying to live a good life trying to live the life of Riley and trying to live a life with a good career my brother wants me to make dolls, something that I'm not too interested in because I can do hard any old day of the week but learning something you you don't always do every day. So let's think about this I'm 33 years old I cannot cook but I'm learning to cook and I'm enjoying it for the first time whatever is when I was 12 and I learned how to cook it was horrible I guess I was too young to appreciate it the same thing with the math and some of the other sciences other than astronomy. And the same thing with history I had a hell of a time with that school until I grow up a little and learn to appreciate it through this vegan tower in Xinjiang China Where do all the pictures can do and make you wanna open your windows to the world.

Like the Beacon Tower Instant Jones China that was left over from the Honda Esty I am still a beacon of hope and he had a be kind of danger it depends on how you see me if you want I can be a beacon of hope usually I am a beacon of hope but I do worn people of things that to come. Usually it's not enemies or anything but it's just bad times I warn people about as far as being a beacon of hope I try to be again a decent human being and a nice person. And I succeed in doing that usually I am very unique and creative and polite. Something that is very rare in these days and people look at me and they say that's a rare person usually in their own eyes they don't sometimes saying there's some idiots that do snicker at me and laugh and I tell them to fly a kite more Lassana polite terminologies for half off. So instead I decide I decide not to get angry I decided to take it up with karma instead and karma deals with it instead of me and my temper that's what I do. And it's a very rare thing to see someone still believe in karma and still trying to be head above water I mean. There's not very many levelheaded people these days are some that are still there but it's a rare find a find someone who is nice and levelheaded down to earth and decent. Something that you don't see every day these days now you just see people with blonde hair blue eyes and big anatomies for girls and forgot his muscles and short hair usually is not the authentic locks and everyone looks for it's a word what iPhone is that I every time I talk to someone they say well I'm glad I've met you you've been a breath of fresh air and me paraphrasing that fear. I am that a beacon of hope somebody who has been through a lot of rough times but still stays who they are something you don't see every day usually usually begins or warnings instead or nothing at all in this fathers society in this society is not very moral these days they allow kids to go on the street and be criminals and stuff instead of teaching them to be in school and stay in school I stayed in the school even though it was at the skin of my teeth and I went with all honors. Even though I had to take a 10 year break or 13 year break from the school life I still start find my Gonzales stayed who I was to begin with. It's not very often you find someone who will go around with pink hair purple hair whatever mohawk pixie cut whatever is not something you see or someone with their natural hair color. If you if you're lucky enough. Instead you find a Lotta Britney Spears look-alikes and a lot of Kenndall look-alikes ken dolls as in the canon Barbies you don't see very many yeah Marilyn Manson's or very many people that are going to be themselves and say what they have to say I find that we shouldn't be after people like Marilyn Manson or the Insane Clown Posse instead I think we are being more compassionate to them because you're just trying to say what really is what we're supposed to be so there are more of a beacon of hope than you think because they actually reach out to the people that are at risk and tell them be yourself do what you have to do and go about life and enjoy life that's what I find with Marilyn Manson in the insane clown posse in boondocks is that that's what it is beer shelf stick to your guns stand up for yourself follow your passions and enjoy life. This is something that we don't see every day anymore and I find if I see a goth person or an email or a punk person I am very lucky because everyone looks the friggin same usually and they is really getting to be a boring world there's not very many gods pongs email or seen people there's not very many people who are ethnic anymore they all look the same blonde and is pretty sad and the people who stick out who dare they stick out usually are the ones that suffer like I have suffered plenty of times but I have stuck with my guns and stayed with what I believed in and what I was interested in in the first place never really Strang from the six year old kid that I was only just more mature and more adult like but still having the same interests having fun doing astronomy learning reading writing art photography music and stuff you know the drill. So it's just a sensor you have to have a sense of self you have to have a good mother and father something some people don't usually have these days I've had a wonderful pair of adoptive parents who taught me to be myself and stick to my guns and be stubborn as hell. Did we always get along no especially me and my father we used to yell at each other but that's beside the point they told me what was the good in the world and that's that something you don't see every day with people like you see most people of broken homes over there with divorced parents usually pretty sad or they're in the system or something it's not fun for this person born in this case with me I was lucky enough to find and I'm not trying to rub it and find the right parents I have mentioned many times to my parents they annoy me they were the ones that I chose to be my parents the birthparents idiots one and two were only chosen for physical attributes my physical strength and physical endurance and flexibility. In other words I have the ability to pick and choose who is going to be my parents I've heard of this with Manny spiritually Give people usually with people who have been on the spectrum are usually a very sensitive and a spiritual way and are very clairvoyant or psychic and they in this case with me I'm still on the spectrum even though I have PTSD I still believe that these abilities I have like I'm an empath and a clairvoyant and a light worker because I on I am on the spectrum..... this might sound silly you're out of Farah Farah sure out of Stephen kings dream catcher but these we got these people like me who are very spiritually gifted I was always told and I knew when there was an asshole around the corner or a good person around the corner or if someone was having a good day or bad day or if they were in pain or if they were happy or whatever an empath and I was able to see the people that were from the other side of the spiritual curtain in my dreams usually so that made me clairvoyant. And I consider myself a light worker a beacon of hope as well because I say beer shall be who you are if you see something like a ghost or whatever just say so if someone says you're crazy it's on them they're the crazy ones not you that's what I learned over my 33 years of living on this sphere. And there is a truth if someone calls you crazy or a spaz out or the r world it's on now The,not you. Like the Beacon Tower in Cintron China leftover to rock I was now a beautiful something surreal and beautiful something that people come to see and admire now just like the Kucha Beacon Tower. Unique different surreal beautiful a beacon of hope not just a beacon of warning.

Airport security

Because of what happened to me as a kid and my brute strength and flexibility and the ability to get on my feet quickly I thought one at one point that I would be in airportsecurity or TSA of CATSA, CATSA is the Canadian version of the TSA is Canadian air transport security authority similar to customs. I was very fascinated with her because I was always in and out of airports a kid. Some thing that I didn't take lightly I enjoyed flying and I enjoyed travelling this was before Covid. After Covid I didn't really like the airport I thought it was a vector for disease were still need to be protected. Anyway I enjoyed travelling it's because of my Uighur ancestors and my Tibetan ancestors and I am also a nomad

I am want to be someone who would travel around I was a good traveller as a kid and I enjoyed it very much so and I still would be a good traveller FYI card. If my aunt didn't hide my silly citizenship card that is so that was that. But it was something that I am still passionate about whenever I get angry at the world is airport security. It's something that I think it's essentially an important is pink hair girl you're thinking gonna be CATSA you gotta be joking me well I'm glad something to say it can happen one day but that's not what I was meant to be on this plan for I was meant to be gentle and helpful to people. What time you get me to work wake up box and brakes and I couldn't get a hold of myself at the time to go in there for security but I did enjoy reading about it and learning about the different groups that are causing the problems in the world I no one was predominant in my life and I'm not gonna mention that he killer group. But anyway I was very yeah grateful that I was in the country and still in the country where there's airport security a decent airport security where you can actually turn around and breathe and not get killed over breathing like you are now Afghanistan and Pakistan instead you were able to go and live your life and not get in trouble but I feel with the elections going on that things are going to change that these little screwup's are going to continue on and pile driver side actual country into the ground I fear. That's why I don't vote because it's just going to invite more problems. I've heard yes you have to vote blah blah blah blah but that's beside the point if I want this country to be secure I will not vote. Because in Romania the voted the dictator or fucked up romania in the first place. Think about it.
There is a war in Ukraine because of someone voting the wrong person in and know not just the Chechen but the Ukrainian have to suffer. Those are also my my ancestors the Chechens and the Ukrainians, they showed up in my DNA test well will in ancestry ca. if it could be a hobby I would go into airport security in a heartbeat. Why because there's too many kids that are out there like me that have been threatened with my wife in other countries and have lived in Third World countries because of violence as well so I believe me if I could and I Ward I would volunteer to be in airportsecurity easily very quickly that's not a joke or pawn on anything this is the real deal if I could and I told my father that one Tony try to tell my mother he said Sufi airport security I don't think so and they ended up having a big fight about it. I still remember that day when I told my father tell my mother I want to go to airport security and try to get rid of the idiots that are ruining the planet and she had nothing to do with what he said because he did something reckless before that caused her to get angry so she was not hearing it so she had to hear it from me years later then I'd be more suited for airportsecurity than anything else but then again anything that involves protecting or say helping people would be very good for me. That's why I want to do what I want to do now because if I can I can not reverse the traumas but I can at least help ease them or lift the weight on the peoples shoulders and help them with a more bearable life that's what I think. That's why I want to be in airportsecurity and now I'm doing these courses and I want to help people who suffer from trauma and EOS in a more positive note and more happy lifestyle and more realistic lifestyle instead of being sad all the time or the price range as there's other emotions you can feel I also father have a lot of trauma in my life and I've lived a happy decent life because I decided to be creative about things whether it be writing this book or reading or writing or producing artwork or something I always do something that's good. The only thing I've only done that was the worst thing on the planet was dent my parents car that was a one time and that was just to get the right diagnosis and my father was not too happy that day and I still remember telling that story in this book. I am not one for loud noises unless it's a concert or a baseball game or a football game or monster trucks I'm not fond of balloons popping in smoke alarms beeping those drive me completely wild hey is that is what real suffering can me sometimes if you don't know for sure.
Same religion teacher that was a pain in my butt in the 11th grade was also a godsend she said Sufi you have to have more compassion for people. Room rings truly have to have compassion and give back to the world in the same way so I believe that it's important to be compassionate as well as giving back you can't be a mean

of grudge and say all I want to give back to the world why no one wants you to be curmudgeon think about down. I still that was the only time that teacher was ever a human to me. And I still sang back to the conversation she said that girl that was bullying you was having a bad day you should've had more compassion so calling her an F in moly. So I decided not to know to look over the bullying but I looked over what she was doing to other people as well and I told her to stop it and I told her if she needed to talk she can talk to someone else instead of bullying the hell out of me and other people I remember that girl her name was Alex again the same girl that said that Saddam Hussein should've been executed ridiculous. With her she always had a bad day.

Talent night

What up getting my first shot an autographs that the talent night I remember exactly, It was old country songs the kind of country I do like to listen to not the new stuff that the new stuff is more white supremacist I find and I don't like that kind of crap is the new country is white power more less. Do me iPhone the old countries are inclusive two all races and religions and also other orientations whereas the new country is heterall and white and Christian I don't like to be mean but that's why it is and I can't stand it. But the very first autograph I got was from Patty and Albert who were part of the country Hall of Fame and they were not of the white supremacist country crap but I actually old country the old-school good stuff like Nancy Sinatra and Johnny Cash country those are the good country I was listening to and I enjoyed it very much that night. It's the new stuff you have to watch out for but anyway I remember getting their autograph they said they're going to get me one of their free CDs as well as I'm going to have a performing talent night next time when I go with my steel tounge drum. I don't think anyone's gonna ask for my autograph worth the steel Toungedrum Heney anyway I got an autograph an even tell my musician can sense another musician even though I'm a rapper I still Saul at the end of the autographs that said best of luck. That must've meant something really special to me because it was some thing that I framed and I enjoyed it still have it facing my bed so I can go to sleep at night looking at it and enjoying the memories of that night hopefully I can enjoy some more good times on talent noise again and I will be able to perform as well this is not a drill anyone this is a real thing. Yes I did need a country Hall of Famer and his wife as well as getting a lot of grass and might get the CD what I'm also going to frame as well I still have to frame my baseball Autographs as well so that's pretty good I still have to do that and then I'll be memorabilia ready. The baseball game in the talent night or not the only time when I have had autograph signed mine hour had to take pictures taken by celebrities I remember one Susan

agluekark, Who was a Inuit singer in a first nation Senior who was very good I love her music told her I loved her music had a picture taken with her this was 10 years ago at this time and then I went to get an autograph as well but then the flood happened three years ago which kind of messed my life and made me a little angry. Because I lost two good autographs but anyway I was able to gain four autographs two from the baseball game the other from the actual concert/talent show.
I still remember getting my picture taken with the framed autographs from the talent night I felt like I got my MD in the state of autograph I was so proud of them I mean.
Yes I knew new tand and car to find if I go to performances and stuff that I try to meet the celebrities in the concert or whatever kind of outing I'm in because I enjoy life enjoy meeting new people I wouldn't have these Golden Sands if it weren't for the bad things that happened yet again in my life.
As one rapper $.50 said in his song album bag for Mercy he said there is no joy without paying no love without hatred so there's something pointy and about that and I say that very much and I know that was a song called many men as an it was very interesting I still listen to that song whenever I feel in the dorms and I tell them without paying the rent no joy. Which is something that I find very honest and true and then I also with Snoop Dogg that he said if you pick up the pieces you'll be tougher than lather that was something I heard and still listen to this time when I didn't and I believe that if you pick up the pieces and take the pain you'll get the joy instead of just hang your enjoy life as well and be tougher than leather I can't do two rappers ideas and mix them together to make him one thing without paying there is no joy and if you don't have the pain you are not tougher than leather.
Which is important for me to think it's important for you to sing to these hip-hop stars or not just blowing the smoke or blown hard air just to say stupid stuff they actually do mean stuff that's important like without pain there is no joy Mira member there was a Ja Rule album called love is pain which is also poignant because love can be painful at times if you let it be but then I can be joyous to if you want to be again the 50 Cent thing. So I believe that these musicians even the metal musicians like old tap Samaya and others are pretty good at talking about was important in life trying to call been trying to help heal yourself and try to be tougher than leather is really important for me to display those in the story that is my story that I'm gonna tell you that it is not over with Jesse and I still have a few more chapters to go. Not Smith figuratively but also really I am not going to let anything I'm gonna be tougher than leather whether anyone likes it or not not everyone likes leather some new. Try to think about this one for a second is it not everyone likes everyone not everyone way to everything so it's important to be to each their own way tougher than leather even though if you don't wear the garment. I find that is important to be very truthful as well and very creative so that's why I'm writing a story to tell you about my little life of mine the life of Sufi who is Sophie Mustafa now Sufi Nelson. Who won back to being Sufi Mustafa I'm back to being Susie Mustafah now because of the dream I had a lucid dream of the prophet peace be upon him. So I decided to go back to the Mustafa. But that's one thing that I find is true to me.
I remember reading about Mustafa for me one of the 99 names of Mohammed peace be upon him again that it means chosen one in Arabic. Something that I believe I was chosen for some good reason for helping other people and to help other people be themselves as well as to be in the safe zone and sometimes to get out of the safe zone if they need to.

Wierd

I remember asking if my mother my adoptive mother was my birth mother and she said no that the woman who go to Cine was way in Eastern Europe near the Middle East. I was shocked and then she said it was also Warzone that I was and I was shocked even more but it explain a lot of my hatred with balloons and smoke alarms certain types of meat and certain taste and smells. Not that my brain blocked out any of what happened to me as a baby but this is what she told me of her side of the story. Oh she was going to sleep all night that's as usual and she had a lucid dream were an angel and I'm pretty sure it was Gabriel was going around telling her there was a girl in Romania that needed some help the angel actually said that from its mouth or his or her mouth Gabriel and said that you have to raise his child and help this child. And I wanted one angel Moron Gabriel and kill I grew older and I started being 30 years old and I started having prophecies on my own some people still think I'm a little lulu about the prophecies but that's beside the point one time I talked to my mom on the phone was in them it was in the middle of the night so it was dark so I was just telling her about a good dream I had and then my whole room light up with a white light this is one time and I figured it was Gabriel every time I turned around away from the source of the light it would come back on as if it was someone's flipping a switch but no switches were being flipped and there was no one in my room except me. So that was a sign of the angel that my mother was talking about was Gabriel that was giving her acknowledgement of my existence and telling me to come for me and help me. That it was the first year the first person that ever help me in my life everyone else outside of my shower in my childhood never really helped me except for when I moved out of my house that's when I really got the help I needed do I think the people at my place have angels telling them that I am coming around now but I know my mother had that dream. And I'm always whippersnapper I'm always smart sometimes I do stupid stuff but I do I do make up for it in the end and I always make sure I MoveOn from the stupidity there is more to it than that you have to be more of an action person than a word person I find. That's what I think and that it's important to go around not judging people for their abilities or whatever. If I saw someone ragging on my friends I would completely go werewolf on them and tell him to buzz off and that would be the polite way of saying it because I don't like people who attack people with disabilities it's not right iPhone I find that anyone who goes after someone with PTSD or whatever disability there is gas a knuckle sandwich in their mouth. That's the only time and I'm not peace loving used in the very peace loving person and I'm very honest and caring but if you don't check yourself before you wreck yourself and you ruined my day or my friends do you have a problem that's basically it. I follow this cold as well the Moshito cold and that means if anyone messes with anyone that they should me have no business telling off like people with disabilities or people with whatever problem they might have well let's just say that person who's mean gets the business from me and they get two middle fingers from me that's the way it goes. Because I don't believe in picking on someone who you who cannot defend them selves or verbalize for themselves in fact I think it's important not to be judge mental. I've been judged so many times because of my phone disabilities and my own problems that it's not even funny and I despise judge mental people and people that discriminate on other people. There is a saying in the world of the insane clown posse we do not see ability race or religion we just see juggalo. And we have this sign is called fuck your rebel flag, for the haters and the haters we called seconds. And if we ever go around finding a hater Waze called chicken hunting usually it's by accident chicken hunting with me are usually try to be friends with someone and then they randomly either block me or they are being an a hole and the next thing you know I just saw it I'm going to say OK

you're a chicken and that's it no so I go chicken hunting and I usually go chicken hunting on Facebook because that's where the idiots usually are. Not that Facebook is in a good side but it's a sometimes a waste of time sometimes sometimes it's good to store your memories but other than that it's not very useful. So I decided I just post my achievements my selfies and stuff and I said I don't really talk to the people because I never know you might be chicken Huntin me and you might be finding a hater. And I know behind every successful person or successful wicked clown in this case there's always a pack of haters there's always I remember Marilyn Manson saying the value you have is not of the love you have but for the people that John you because you're better than them. That's what I think about this whole situation with cyber bullying on Facebook and stuff that I am worth more than the people that bully me and attacked me or block me randomly for no reason it's not nice but I'm better than them because I don't hide behind a computer and say stupid stuff for the stupid stuff. When you're on the Internet there's an etiquette you don't block people for random reasons phantom reasons more likely and you don't go around spreading hate and you don't show your anatomy to people that don't want to see it particularly people who are not doctors so that's another little no no I've had to tell people is like put it back in where it belongs in it or I cut it off.
It's called this is what I call safe Internet is my not interacting with these people or minimally interacting with these people unless they're penpals and I'll get started on penpals pretty soon. Penpals or a different story they're more friendly and less likely to be a pain in your.....

Penpals

Penpaling is when you send a letter or email to someone you don't really know but do you have that trust with him because you are a match to OSM are you make a connection with them. And they usually are from another country or another part of the country. That's just the idiot saying for a penpal. In other words I correspond with people from Africa Asia Europe south and Central America I do a lot of good things in order to get penpals and I find that it's a more positive experience emailing a penpal or talking to a penpal or riding the ladder instead of going on Facebook and getting BSBS meaning you know what. You are less likely to find her age range in a penpals so I thought you would get on Facebook and the Facebook has peanut gallery and I were you I think we've all been through the peanut gallery. When I penpal I penpal seriously and I actually talk to the people. But I don't bother with people on Facebook as I said in the earlier chapter. What started me on pen palling I'll get a few things going.

Reason one: when I was on a cruise one time there was this waiter who was very nice to me and my family and he always did the right thing for me my garlic pasta something I like garlic it's something that's good for immune system and go ahead to fight diseases and salsa good brain food supposedly as my father said. So I always eat garlic passive plain garlic pasta that's the way I ate as a kid just to

get the IQ I had in the Covid fighting immune system that help me survive Covid in the first place. As you have to eat the right stuff before I get the shots I think anyway I got really friendly what is waiter he said he had a daughter who want to learn English my mom said that would be nice for Sufi to have a pen pal, and since grade 7 to grade 12 I've been pen palling with this girl from Malaysia her name was Fatima she was very nice I enjoyed her letters very much and her gifts but more also reading about her culture and learning about stuff and being her friend I still look for her on Facebook or Penn power or never say that allows pen powerline but I am too of no avail finding her the last time she went to the army and I never heard back from her ever again which makes me think she may have died which is sad but then here's the other reason why I penpal
Reason: I penpal because I want to learn different languages and make new friends as well I think we all know that I started me back on penpal Lake was an app called penpal world which is now is sage I enjoy going on the site penpal world and seeing who is interesting and who is not or going on a girl penpal and seeing who I might do they come up with as my match for a penpal or slowly is very fine slowly is an app that is supposed to be like snail mail but it's very interesting because it's like more like email by slough. So I enjoy that and that got me back in the pen palling I've been pen palling for years and years and years after I lost my original penpal Fatima.
I do more panpaling that I do anything else I'll lose in writing and reading and art and photography and Netflix I do a lot of different things but I love penpaling whether be through email or snail mail is fun and interesting to get to know these people and their cultures some of them are my ancestral cultures which is even better. I find that it's important to connect with the world especially parts of the world that you belong to as well not trying to be nasty or anything but Connect with who you belong with and learn from who you don't belong with and that's basically Ed and then we will belong with each other that's what I find with society would be a lot easier if we penpal a lot that we would be more excepting of each other if there was more penpals going around but people finally cellular start they use Facebook for a space for me or some other stupid side. Which really sets my gold on fire that mean it's like whatever happened to email or WhatsApp or snail mail.
As I said I only use Facebook is promote my music and that's the final straw or my heart or whatever I do that I enjoy and that's it and I really could care less about the peanut gallery I always have the finger emoji app ready and we're ready to go for the peanut gallery and a heart emoji ready for the people around the world who are my penpal so let's just think about it peanut gallery gets the finger the rest of the world gets a heart. And that's basically because I believe that if you have a phone number on email will email you most likely going to be true blue instead of with Facebook you can make a fake account really easy and that's the scary part with Facebook I find. I despise Facebook from the beginning I didn't mind the Avs it had at first but I didn't like it because there's so many idiots in there still are and I let them not get through to me now but when I was younger forget it I am emotional wreck.
Then I saw it on Facebook I saw it was a penpals right on Facebook which was Korean Muslim which I try to join thinking I was going to find penpals instead I got a whole Load of bs and hatred, why because I was non-binary and it was being at the same time as a Muslim they didn't think that was right they didn't think I should wear jewellery and stuff when idiot even said that he knew where I live yeah right and I still try to get this particular group taken down because it's a hate group how do I hate speech and extremism and even as much as child smart ass fine that's why I find when I Rylo can I find something worse and worse and worse on there on that particular freaking group has a bunch of crackheads.

Ghost :memory

One thing I remember and this is when I was in the fourth grade I was sitting on the swing set just swaying in the swing shed and trying to stargaze it was a cloudy night but it was supposed to be soggy. Then I fog rolled in in particular part of my backyard where the dog that I called a patch used to be buried in soon enough I was frozen with fear paralyzed and then I found out that I see the operation of all the form of a black lab. That's when I just saw that was a ghost and I snapped out of my paralysis and ran like the dickens and decided I was going to tell my mother she heard me screaming and said what the Hecks going on. I told her there was a ghost in the backyard the ghost of the dog Jennifer the name Jennifer was the dog. See you anymore leave me and I said well I was a frog and smoke and then an apparition of the dog something I don't usually see all my time. It was really hard wrenching to see my mom and hear my mom and say you don't talk silly that's nonsense try to sell my father still the heart wrenching Rizal don't talk Shelley is there's no such thing as ghosts but there are there was a sword I saw for real and it was the real deal and I was very paranoid the ghost was gonna come back even though the ghost was of a friendly Anthony still it was scary. I ended up deciding to keep my mouth shut for most of my childhood after that whether I saw a ghost or whatever I ended up keeping it to myself keeping everything pent-up and just like going to the bathroom I ended up having to go real bad and ended up having to blow my stack when I blew my stack that was when I am going what is the therapy I told the therapist everything that I saw from the dog aberration she never judge me to the UFOs that my father was calling about one time I don't know why you didn't believe in ghost but then believe in UFOs I was beside the point but anyway I talk to the nurse and I open up very quickly and then pretty soon I opened up to my parents and I told him exactly what I thought about them that they were a pain in my butt and that they have cramp my style and that they ruined more or less my childhood by telling me I talk silly or horrible things. I ended up having to say one time to my mom go fly a kite In other words go F yourself.
And my parents had to take my abuse from my own mouth they didn't like it they rebottle many times and I told him to shut the hell off it's my turn to talk now that they send their opinion which is silly and I told him that they were silly and stupid wasn't my finest moment with my parents but anyway I had to say listen there are ghosts there are these things around that are real and you are stupid enough not to think they're real. So that's why I decided not to be like my parents who are close minded I want to be open minded who knows you could see siren how do you get to whatever cartoon cat you never know what you might see in the night on this case with me Siren head the daytime.
At least some people have to group don't believe me and I say I see something because they also believe in the same thing my parents never never believed in that and I still rag on my not allowing can you speak my mind instead my parents bought

my love with toys and video games always trying to spoil me so I wouldn't have to remodel again Sam but I did one day at therapy and that was the final they never said another thing to me again that was negative if I said I saw a ghost they believe me that was a day when I put the gauge the ring in my ear which is the ear expander for the first time and they didn't like that and I said well I'm sorry this is why it's going to be like and yes there are ghosts around and stuff. Something they didn't enjoy hearing and they had to hear it and I said it and it was every second one was the F word I believe which I'm not happy about but I had to tell them exactly how I felt about them controlling ways. They were good people but they didn't know how to parent they were more logic-based than anything else and that kind a ruin that for them. It went after the ear expander incident gays earrings we ended up deciding not to talk for a while I stayed in my room playing my video games I watch the stupid TV and I ended up deciding when I decided I was going to talk to them I talk to them and I told him he listen this is just the way I am and if either take it or leave it and they had to take it they actually said that they except. And that was the final thing and ever since then they haven't bothered me in the least unless I didn't do something Cura wise or if I was doing something that was actually stupid. But if I saw something out of the ordinary or if I was doing something that was fast originally they acknowledged it right away because they ended up being very open minded to me because you're one stupid type of earring. It's kind of sad there an earring how to get in the way and get my parents straight now. Now whenever I say Melanson ghost when I was in my home they believed me and they didn't mark the system. I would hate to say that I'm a control freak but that was basically how I had to do it and then of course I said after that oh yes I also reverted to Islam.
That was a tumultuous time and that was the beginning of my first year of the 12th grade as I said they were kind enough after a while to know that I was under a lot of stress over my childhood that they want me to have a good education and they decided to give me split my 12 year of school free school into two. And they decide that I need a break from education and I actually agreed with them but then they had to bring in the twit named Cassandra who's another story all together.

Cass

Cassandra was not the best mental health worker she trying to get on my nerves every time she could one time she said that the Nazis were right to go after my people the Asians not trust the Jewish people I'm not really piss me off because I thought nobody should be experimenting on. And I was very angry and I was very upset to the point where on my mother was about ready to make a complaint it was in January 2019 or 2020 I cannot exactly remember but I do remember that he said that horrible thing about Mangolie saying that the agents have coming out of the well as a Jews to be exterminated an experimented on something that triggered me very much so I was mad than I ordered I wanted to punch her right there in the car right in her jaw but I didn't want to do anything to get in jail Cuz she was a scumbag. But it was getting worse than that when I ended up going to the group home she ended up getting in between me and my mother when I just started to reconcile between me and my mother and tell my mother that Mohamady the isis bastard was no longer around.

He will want to say every time I try to do a new piercing and I yes I tried to pierce myself for est that I reasons and for reasons of ancestry cultural but not to hurt myself he was livid and every time I call my mom she say oh every time you call your mommy end up doing a new piercing I was like that is a pile of shit excuse my language word that was the truth told my mom she had many times where she said this Cassandra person was a piece of work I try to avoid her calls and texts as much as possible not my mother Cassandra 30 hours just to avoid her bullshit.

Soon I ended up walking around trying to deal things on my own this was the beginning of the pandemic 2021 or 12,020 I don't know I fucking don't know but I was so mad at the time and I was like leave my mother out of this and then she had to go look at the end of this DBT program which was more theoretical and more pain in the ass than it is mindfulness she was really a pain in my arse. I didn't enjoy having to deal with her at least once one time I try to avoid DVT just to avoid her but one of the water pressure you have to go to the program or you're gonna be stuck with her for the rest of your life and I said OK I'll go this one's in after that I never heard from her again until I had a series of nightmares it was a year after I threatened Mohamady with the authorities and then I ended up saying hey listen I've been having these nightmares about my mothers friend let's say and he was hurting me. That was about it then she decided to re-open my fucking file and say that I had to talk to her again after that after the nightmare stopped I didn't talk to her she never talk to me and I was younger but she left quite a scar on me because she has always tried to westernize me and try to make me fluid and such and stupid and everything else is good she did it did nothing good for making a horrible human being. I would give her and give you the last name of this Twitternipple but now I would be a breach of my confidentiality personal confidentiality especially if this person is going to end up in jail.

When I said to the workers in my house was it Cassandra was racist she was biased against my mother because of what she did to my father and many other stupid things I try to keep a bullet journal and stuff and try everything to keep her out of my hair that Cassandra that is.

Siri how far is able to break free a few months ago maybe a year ago I was able to get away from her and I never talk to her again I might decided blocker off my phone because I don't want her to be in my life anymore he was a horrible man a lot of workers he was judge mental and very disturbed I mean if anyone says in the Asians had it coming as well as the Jews in the most were people that were hurt in the holocaust then I guess they are disturbing very Marshall. And she even called me a sand ****** and other names that I'm not Gonna to say.

One time when I was with Leah she said that this Cassandra person was a neo Nazi as well as a crackhead that should've been a warning sign that Cassandra was not a good person to begin with trying to westernize me trying to make me who I am not. She was not very smart for that way I cleared on her job a lot better and that's not why I am going into this line of work I'm going in this line of work because it's important to help people but what are the points he could've done a better job at her job that is Cassandra. She was a real piece of work she always has something to say that was negative and I despise.

I might be buying non-binary and then I might be actually pan which is fine which is true maybe I don't know I'm still trying to figure out myself in this world but anyway the non-binary part was true anyway I don't believe that you should be telling people what to do and trying to westernize non-western people inside except people as they are and who they are bracelet I called her I was trying to teach her my cultures that I belong to and she threw them in my face and said no you're gonna be rational as you want to handle it the white man way as if I was like an indigenous person in the old days where I hate to say this year residential schools it was horrible. That's why I was like assimilation is assimilating me into western

society white society which I didn't wanna have any part of. Exactly what the people did her brother and they're doing indigenous people Wayback win and still to this day I despises so much this kind of racism does assimilation.
That's when I decided to say ha ha assimilation and assimilation was nothing more than racism in genocide in his own way it's trying to kill off the persons soul and culture similar to what happened to the First nation people in can out which I don't agree with either kind of assimilate people and trying to tell them to be white it's not right be who you are in the first place who God created you to be. I guess she was just being with the devil create in her to be Cassandra that is.

Post cass

Post Cassandra I've been doing pretty well I've been much happier with my life and with my life and my behaviours in general I haven't had one the last time I had a "temper tantrum like what I would call a temper tantrum temper tantrum what happened two years ago and that it was either a flashback or just something out of the whack a day but other than that it's not because of somebody pulling the strings on my brain telling me to assimilate. That's what Cassandra was trying to do and post Cassandra I still am who I am to this day I am resilient I am what I am supposed to be in the first place who I am Sophie Mustafa that's who I'm supposed to be and Cassandra was nothing more than a thorn in my side and when he was gone and behaviour stopped and I haven't really blown a gasket really and if I did I would go and use it to make money to clean the decks or shovel the snow or clean my at my job either way I use my anger for the productive things instead of just flying off the handle.
I am very depended on my job meeting the people that hire me depend on me to do my job and do it well and I'm very proud that they very honoured that they allow me too clean their house and I'm very proud that they and honoured that they depend on me to clean that's very good I would do it for free but I had to do have to have tattoo money for tattoos away yet a job and be sorry just getting to that part of my time when I need a job anyway just to get some experience so I why the heck not. But I am honoured that they say that they depend on me to clean their house which I'm glad about. I do a very good job I just get a little annoyed before I do the job and then I do the job well and thoroughly using my anger as a way of cleaning up house and using it to my advantage getting money and getting work experience instead of ruining my day. That was the same thing last year when I was working at a summer camp I would just get a little annoyed and then start cleaning the hell out of the summer camp. I've been known as the best cleaner there is around I think that's what I've heard you're a good cleaner the best cleaner I've seen etc. etc.

And I know that was a compliment so that I accept and enjoy. And what comes out of it is something beautiful a tattoo and maybe a piercing by a professional always buy a professional because it's easier to take care of that way if it's done by a professional I have done by yours truly. Like if I had to do my own tattoos I would be doing Polysporin as well as the moisturizer and that would not be good aftercare and I would have a bad tattoo if I did it my way but since I had done professionally it's just slap on the moisturizer don't get it wet try to use sensitive soap when washing it in a way you go I moisturize it once a day to three times a day three times a day one is fresh ink and then after that I increase gradually from three times a day I called the moisturizer my tattoo feed. And that's what I use my anger for is to get tattoos and piercings not that I have piercings but you know what I mean one in the same come together and I take care of it very well take pride in it and as well as I also work hard for the thought of working hard and only to work hard. Something my parents try to instill in me but didn't really work out until I left the house that's when I started to actually learn how to work hard and do a good job other than when I was in high school.
I have four tattoos that I have water like a dog for a good dog not like a forest I've been very happy to have worked these jobs still working one of these jobs and hopefully we will get another job at some point. And I'm very interested in getting more tattoos and seeing what other values I can learn from another job to. You never know what food has in store so that's why I keep waking up every day is something new and it can be positive or negative if you choose wisely it can be positive choose wisely my friends.
Since I left my original home I haven't really had a bad day except when I had to deal with Cassandra but that was Paul pre-Cassandra ordering Cassandra but no polish Cassandra I've been flourishing like a wildflower spreading all over the grass I've been nothing but the best sure I may have had my option that I was still I've been it's your flourishing you're well. And I'll and I have a done a lot of things without Cassandra's help. Where is with her what was I doing piercing my own flash to make a piercing and one really should've been a professional it should've done it that's the size of it and I ended up going to the freaking hospital one day I still owe the woman who caught thc what I call a mini staff infection a lifesaver and I still owe her my life. As for the doctor she said either take out the piercings that I made or get a tetanus shot I said I'm taking the darn things out. And I swore against piercings and less it was donc professionally and when I had my first tattoo done professionally and I saw how easy it was to take care of it then I started thinking maybe I'll try to see if someone can someone who is a professional emphasis on professional wanna do a piercing or three and that would be hard and I would be done with the piercings I'm done with that have your face full of metal remember that last year as if it was yesterday I would be hating his last year's problem and I still tell people to this day I do not do it yourself I hate all the words do it yourself or DIY I hate it sometimes it's not a bad thing but to me it's the flu. Because I almost had a staff infection at one point from my own stupidity trying to pierce my Medusa.

Patience

One thing I've learned with this COVID-19 is a little bit of patience can go along way sometimes I'm still impatient and one things right away you gonna ask many people around me sometimes I am zen and I'll be completely nice as 90% of the time 10 Percent of the time I can be a real pain in the butt still want it comes to patients but it's a work in progress. Why do I have to be patient during the pandemic because I needed I wanted to get tattoos and I wanted to shop still get open again and I wanted a lot of other things and I had to order from Rocky, So that was boring patience is ordering things to snail mail is not just penpals but also waiting until the tattoo shops are open for you to go around to get your tattoos and it was well worth my wait. I believe that a little bit of patience is important but you cannot be too patient or zone. But I believe that is important to be patient in some cases why he can't be controlling control freak he or weird about things.
Three almost 3 years of stupid stupid that's a soccer ball Zazai college and I even and it up with the stupid batch of soccer balls. Yes I am at that was cove in 19 one time and had to stay downstairs I practice my steel tongue drum and weighed the 10 days out of the minimum of 10 days and even did my ukulele that ukulele is a little hard on me but the steel tongue girl was gonna couldn't do the guitar because I involved singing and my singing voice is still on the Fritz. But I am good with a rapping voice in other words I was able to rap and I am now a rapper because of that and three years almost 3 years I dreamt of getting my first tattoo and when I got the first tattoo was like plunging into a swimming pool like as if you're a little kid it was fun it was exciting refreshing. That's what happens when you wait your turn and wait why do you were supposed to be waiting. That's what I find.
There are sometimes during the pandemic I was not too happy especially the part of me getting the soccer balls and admitted it does look like a pair of freaking soccer balls a bunch of freaking soccer balls that's why it is that's what they are a bunch of idiot soccer balls that you look like soccer balls and act like soccer balls and they didn't in the wave your breathing and stuff is very awful. Good cold drink was the only option I had to get rid of a cough when I had the Covid. And I always took a cold drink and I always drank particularly lemonade lemons orange orange juice and yoghurt those are always good for your immune system. And the fact that I hat a childhood of eating nothing but garlic, (man I love that stuff) How to help me survive I don't credit the vaccines even though they helped a little bit but they only help a little bit that's all they do and they they keep coming up with new strangers of stupid soccer ball and the new friggin vaccines and it's getting annoying so I just suck on a lemon that's what I did in front of TikTok one day the day when I was diagnosed with Covid I saw Donna Ramen for three minutes enjoying every minute of it the lemon was good but the Covid was a pain in my throat particularly I was ready for a neck tattoo full neck tattoo by the time it was over with because my throat was so scratchy and I got a scratch my side of my neck and it still doesn't hurt. I've never really had any problems with having to

go to the hospital or anything why because I'm a tough cookie and I eat properly particularly I'm a tough cookie. I'm horny my people have been exposed to these little I'm sorry to say this bastard's for centuries and centuries and now at my genetics has saved me again the only time on it hasn't saved me was with the stupid razor Kinda do a pixie cut. That's about the size of that.

I was very good spirit even though I was annoyed what's the soccer balls. And pretty soon I was able to get back on my feet really quickly. There is another time I healed quite quickly I will my ankle it took a week for it to heal instead of mines do usual months for someone else took a week for me but that's because I knew what what pain wise the bells and I said no I'm going to use the Walkingstick for the mailbox and I use a Walkingstick for the mailbox and after 24 hours no Walkingstick. That is the weirdness of my body and we are now showing all. And I was being very patient about my ankle I was like trying to toy turn it away and turn it around trying to get back to gather again like I used to do with Paul Masson and it worked with and patience. Patients can be a painful thing but when you have a high pain tolerance yourself you can take it sometimes when you don't see it coming you better pack her up that's all I can say is that when you have a side pain having patience is something you have to see, or you're in a world of hurt Pokora that's all I can say about that is pucker up that's the same with pain Covid or patients if you can see it coming your way you can actually thought away and destroy it but if you don't see it coming and you act like a baby Lala then you end up in a world of hurt and that's basically the truth at all. I do not act like a baby Lala when I had my tattoo(s) did not after four when I had Covid and didn't act fool during the pandemic after the COVID-19 problem with me Asia the pandemic was over for me and I was done I still wear the masks just to be considerate and kind and compassionate to other people and that's why it is because you never know I could have it again but I'm just saying that I have an expression.

I don't want to believe in spreading disease and I am also thinking about riding to the Prime Minister to close the airports except for freight and packages because of the Covid I find there's a lot of ignorant people that are travelling around without masks or otherwise and it just drives me stark raving mad at some people don't wear their masks in crowded spaces makes you want to pull out my natural hair out. It's like where are the damn thing or go home I'll be in a little area and don't wear it and you can be fine one of the to go home and not be in a crowd spot or not wear it in the world area that's all I don't see I don't see it as going into a public Spartans crowded and not wearing a freaking mask. That's enough for me to get my mouse one in full speed and I'm not even get started because it'll be just F this an F that.

I am the girl with the pink hair that usually she not bottle pink Mark Twain paying because I'm tired of waiting on toxic chemicals I'm also sick and tired of toxic emotions I've had mixed emotions all my wife I'm the pink hair girl. Do I need this for a tension no I do this to sell express myself and to express my uniqueness in life just like my tattoos and piercings I'm not meant to say oh look at me I'm tattooed and pierced look at me and I I'm just here trying to exist and trying to express myself in my own way it's called freedom of expression is in the chart of rights and freedoms very much so and even in the UN and progressi and freedoms that you should be able to enjoy the freedom of expression to an extent unless you go wrong with assuming hateful stuff on your body like white stuff like white supremacist staff or some but if not it's not offending or hateful then go ahead express yourself as is but do stay within the law I like to believe that I am the pitta me of freedom of speech and freedom of expression. Why because I decide I'm gonna wear what I'm gonna wear how I'm gonna wear it what tattoo I'm going to get what type of tattoo what design and maybe even how many piercings I get but I'm just gonna go with three because as much prettier than 1001 piercings. That's what I think it more is not always more less is more sometimes so I will be going around with salmon roll in two nostril piercing on one side of my nose and I am a new role that would be the size and if I get piercings and even after I even have three earlobes. Three earlobes from a gauging incident that I experienced one time what happened was the earring slipped out of my ear one night after a good nights sleep I found out my ear was split I said I'm not going to fix it there's no fixing it because there's nothing to fix it's who I am to begin with. When I started talking to my brother he said well maybe you should see a plastic surgeon and I said I'll be yours pure and simple told it's not going anywhere or you either one drive you nuts and you go out of the mental hospital or I find another brother either way it's not going away and then my bright and dark really got annoying my doctor and she said oh you I see you have three earlobe do you want them returning the one I said hell no and she said well there is still the option of plastic surgery and I said that's for perfectionist and burn victims and people actually need it I don't need it over to some thing that really is nothing wrong to begin with except three earlobes it something I would put in my profile on plant penpal world as a fun fact I have three-year-olds how many people have three or Lowe's in Lassens natural not very many. So right to me beauty is not really something that society should monitor is for you to enjoy you to express yourself the way you sure should express yourself the way you should and only the way you should you shouldn't try to fit in and try to assimilate or anything else for yourself you what your culture is do you want your nosology is a religion and be who you are don't go around calling to be something you're not just to be beautiful or less to be westernized. I'm a Sufi mistake as well as a Shamaness Lake person as well as middle of a Muslim that's my religion on my Sufi mystic shaman and a teensy bit of Muslim that's what I am and that's what I am to be getting with us how are you starting life - how are you will and then life at age 115 hopefully if not 115 at least a decent enough Asia ISA wow I had a hell of a good life.

I am not going to find the love of my life lol do I really care because in fact romance doesn't mean very much when you can be just friends and I've been told that many times and I have indoctrinated that then I decide if I go on a dating site I say I'm looking for friends only that shit if anything else happens then fine but I'm happy just being friends I don't have to reproduce in order to be happy or healthy. And I know that for a fact. So it's more quality and quantity or the perks in life it's more quality.

I also believe that life is not just about learning but also about enjoying yourself and having a good time you rated style having reading a good book having a good conversation riding stargazing whatever you do that's G rated and fine you don't have to be X-rated or me producing children in order to be happy and if you can find a maid that's fine with you but I can't I'll never be able to because of that guy in high school and I don't really care at this point in my life because I rather be friends with people instead of being an idiot and try to date someone and get my heart broken get in your funk and snap at people. I used to have an indigenous indigenous name in a literacy class I don't know why I was in the literacy class but anyway I was called Sufi snapping turtle. Meaning that they compare me to the snapping turtle I call that my first nation's name because it sounds got to ring to it snapping turtle and it's true sometimes I do snap at people so but anyway I'd rather not snap too much at people and date instead I'd rather be friends and the snapping turtle that only snaps so I didn't eat. I've lived a good 33 years of my life this is noble and I have enjoyed it so far what are we have an extra I don't know but I'll find out when the time comes. This is my first 33 years of my life in a nutshell and this is basically what is my first my first masterpiece not just as a book or a diary or a painting or drawing or tattoo but as my life is not perfect but it's where it is. I am enjoying my life exactly as it is the way it should be the way God intended me to enjoy life little bit of a Lonewolf but with some friends. And I thirst for knowledge That is unquantichable. I can drink manage drinks that are nonalcoholic I don't believe in alcoholic drinks but I do believe in drinking knowledge it as much as and getting drunk off knowledge that's what I think and I find it's more important to be enjoying life is life's too short to be pissed off all the time I remember hearing from the movie American history X. Sorry for the spoiler

I am who I am

Hello my name is Sufi Mustafa I am who I am I am a girl and turn back non-binary who decided not to deal with rice bowl crap but instead to enjoy life as it is and enjoy the things that normal people don't usually enjoy because they have their heads so far stuck up there but anyway. I am an artist authorization photographer rider mediation rapper and I'm also there is a human being and a loving person you're a chatterbox yes but I'm also a good person to be around when you need someone. My hobbies include astronomy stargazing among other things like rap music horror movies Netflix and other things. That's basically me and I shall I may have not had the best of lives again worth but I lived a good life nonetheless in my opinion the best wife I can live the life I live was enjoyable at first no it wasn't but it turned out to be enjoyable and I hope it stays enjoyable for the rest of my life. I am very happy to be proud of who I am proud of where I'm going in life still don't still have an idea but still don't have a clue where I'm going but I have a bit of an idea with my interests Alicia if I could be a astronomy teacher if not may be a worker of some sort tell you how to be a decent person not a woman of the night I'll tell you that much work are meeting someone who helps people and so when I go about my life I think of other people first even when I rap about my problems over Apple about my emotions on the things in the world I just tell it as it is I don't sugarcoat anything I don't sugarcoat sweet ass I just do what I have to do I tell him the truth that's what I am doing in this book my mom Bobby would be very happy to know that I am very interested in telling the truth and being a good person being honest and well groomed human being today.
Am I everyone's best friend not always there are some people that I've been friends were in the can my enemies but together people in my elementary school became my enemies and my enemies had became my friends but that's basically it and I've also had people who just be where enemies to begin with and stayed enemies till the very end. But I don't really care about the enemies I care about the friends and I have

people that care about me and the people I care about invert colours.
This I remember once in great savron is the value of the human life value of your own life too and to be kind to yourself how do I know because some twit ended up with a autopsy video how he got it and garden into the school to show us girls to scare us into not starving ourselves was one thing but I still wonder how he got it what kind of money he had to get it. He must've been working very hard for the money to get it. iPhone is mother knew what he was doing with the money getting an autopsy video to scare girls in the not starving themselves it was kind of a prank but in the way it was a life lesson I never really believe in suicide I never really believe in anorexia even though these are medical conditions I don't believe that they have to be around they can be prevented very easily if you were given the right tools and live in the right guidance in life that's why I don't believe in anorexia and suicide and boulimia I believe in trying to better yourself and trying to help yourself while long does your medication how old" they're still preventable and they will stay preventable if I can help it that's why I don't bother with the bullying that's why I said the bullies are known more than dirt on my feet.
Something that I didn't want to have to say but I had a say here to get what I wanted to express myself the way I wanted to express myself in a healthy way
I also believe in the signed not piss off the fairies meaning don't let her or do anything to harm the environment I believe that you should be very respectful to the planet as is my ancestry and my beliefs I believe that we are to be more respectful towards nature and its planet this lovely sphere. I remember a lot reading a book from Robert Young Powelton same guy that wrote worlds most dangerous places when he said that one place was so dangerous because it was so polluted. And I have always I guess that's where I get my fairy energy from I don't know what else knows from that one book I guess it is because I after reading that book I said never again Wes littering and I have I saw someone littering I tripped him little tramp them and then fall on your face yeah I can be versus when he don't treat the planet properly. If you treat those planet and people properly you don't get tripped up by me. But the one thing you have to watch out for is me I am who I am I am around and I'll be around for quite some time so be careful what you do. I might be a nice girl but I can be, and the skies it depends on how you treat other people around me I don't care if you're of a millionnaire or a bomb if you do not treat people properly you get punched in the face and I don't care what part of the world what kind of law Zarar get what you deserve so I am who I am that's all I can say I am Sufi Mustafa

Poem or two

This hopeis making you frozen what do you want to go and help yourself
This hope will help you go to many places
This hope Will get you out of the emotional doldrums in back in the life if you are willing to embrace it

This hope We have here
This hope we have here
This hope we have here
This Hope we have here

Burns stronger than any fire on the planet even in the devil's pit in
It will never be extinguish like the devils pair Turkmenistan

This hope we have here
This hope we have here
This hope we have here
This hope we have here

Will do more wanders in any medication can if you allow it to
Let's hope we have here can I actually help with your medication
Think about when you have a bad day there is still hope the bear is just non temporary
So there's no point in doing
About it except for hope that tomorrow will be a better day

there is Hope
There is hope
There is Hope
There is hope

And this pawn means a lot to me even in the darkest of times and still like you were in the dark of night there and start it still The stars in the sky and the moon is the sky so think about that. If it's a cloudy day the sun is still out sore or the star is in the mood you just cannot see that. Just think about that hope is always around the corner and hope will always be there for you if you let it be there and I said even if it's dark the stars and moon are out the sun is still out it's just not seeable. The same thing with cloudy days and daylight the sun is out but the star seeable their faded but they're there. Your face and society might when you find what I bought but you find you could I hard and I will bought and and you will never let go. This is what this poem is about actually said it'll do more than one or is there any on medication it can do with medication this poem will do a lot more than just be a bunch of words pretty words words that mean a lot another bunch of words that mean a lot or fidelity bravery and integrity

Alexander the movie

This is what I remember in the 10th grade before I walk Valley janitor the movie is that my father said I look like an Indian from India as in a Hindu or Buddhist. He wasn't trying to be racist running he was just trying to say what I look like and I want in the mirror and look I look Sammy Asian Sammy Middle Eastern is that me why to biracial tri-racial whenever you want to call it so I it's either the way you look at me either the angle or the lighting that determines whether you say I'm white Middle Eastern or Asian. But I didn't think of that as those cultures as being a piercer tattoo happy until I ended up going to see the movie Alexander with my drama class in high school everyone had to go even I had to go on and I try to fake the flu. It turned out it was a good movie I enjoy and recommended everyone and I still do to this point but I don't believe that he have to see it you can be recommended to see. But I highly recommend this movie but anyway I ended up seeing this year at the end in bactria which is now in part of central Afghanistan part of the Himalayan or Tibetan Empire and I ended up finding out that they had at least at the very most three piercings and a whole crap load of tattoos I guess someone was right when they said more is less when it comes to piercings it is more class here and it shows us goddess symbol if you have less than four piercings if you can help it. Because I saw the Hindus have the piercings I seen the Bactrian Champions have the piercings in the movie of Alexander and also the Persians having piercings as well that's what got me interested in expanding my ears not overhearing things I mean stretching my or a longing my earlobes and then I ended up with three year olds because of it but that's beside the point and I ended up enjoying the movie and I said the takeaway was is that I should get and I started to get interested in piercing and tattoos. Yet again in my life it was as if I was a six-year-old girl you saw that first eyebrow ring and said wow that's cool and then had the first rub off tattoo and said damn it I wish it stayed. But I was not going to be fazed by a piddly little rub off tattoo or the fact that I wasn't going to get a piercing yet professionally I was going to do it anyway but anyway that was a takeaway from the movie that those were what my ancestors looked like. And I wanted to go back to the old school getting not rings but finger tattoos the knuckle tattoos in the thumb knuckle tattoos as well as did tattoos in general that are nice looking this a my status as an intellectual. I also believe that I should get three piercings to say that I am at least a brahman.

Do I Believe In the case system of my ancestors know but I do believe that I am a modern-day brahman only wears a pair of girl balls instead of instead of man parts that's what I am a female brahmin.   But unlike the case system of oil in Asia I believe in accepting everybody as they are I don't see a dalit I don't see anything of that unless you're a doctor then you're a dalit in my opinion but that's because you abused my people in WWII as well as the Jewish people in WWII and that makes you a Darrell it is the way you treat other people not your disease or your class

system or what you do for a living less you're a doctor than your a dalit. Why because I don't like talkers the racist and they are horrible human beings I find and they just are blood-hungry seems some of them are even way so some of them are even more even though she's in WWII like mangle. Tamiya lower class human being or subhuman being a dalit is someone who cannot keep their words to themselves in a nice manner but instead Spears our hatred and Grace to other people or does hateful things to other people like human experimentation. So I don't believe that these doctors are really important in life there are important to an extent you don't want to die or go over weight or anything of that matter but then again you do not want them to tell you how to run your life. I find their Dallas more than anything else because they're hateful I've had two hateful doctors in my life dr. O and dr. Rossi both of which are a pain in my ass. And they're just a bunch of dalits. Meaning Outkast in my opinion because they outcast in themselves in World War happen helping with the human experimentation. I don't believe in hatred is a way of being a good person I think hatred is a way of being the complete opposite but there's no love without hate So you you're stuck with it either way we have to have boss but that's beside the point. I decided that I'd rather just stick with love without the hate. There is such a way of doing such a thing as a love without hate without digging bigotry or genocide or anything of that matter.
Just follow your heart you will see that this is what you're supposed to be a human being and only that and you should be treating other people as respect I find the real brahmins are people who are people who treat other people with respect and kindness and decency those are the people that should have access piercings and tattoos and have access money and access everything forget about the people with em deese they're not really really worth a pinch of sand there just anything but a dalit because they're bigots give me a bigot is a dalit or a Outkast untouchable.

Weird places to learn from

The weirdest places I learned from and had an interest in Psychology and mental health before I found out I was mentally ill was from watching serial killer documentaries at in the 1990s and 2000s. I was very interested in Transformers what was going on in their mind and decided to see what was going on. So I also know I don't need picked up law books to read about law but I ended up finding some old Psychiatry books and learn about the brain. I was very interested in what was going on and I said someone is acting funny it's usually there's something wrong with them in the background meaning in their childhood something in their childhood is wrong if they are acting funny. But I didn't know I was only fourteen at the time I started learning more and more as the time going on that it was more than just serial killers that it was just about to motionless and emotional IQ and stuff like that so I decided to broaden my horizons and end up deciding to learn more about other things about society as well and make people go crazy. Unfortunately one of them is ptsd, pgasd to me is just an emotional response that is very misunderstood no. I think it's not a serial killer maker or anything else it depends on how you create your life that didn't matter the most but it also matters if another traumatic event happens I've learned when I learned about these particular people iPhones I learned that they are very interesting and they teach us about how to be human in the first place had to be caring about other people instead of being hateful and evil and deviant. Said we should band together and get rid of the serial killers are still going to learn from them instead and learn and move forward from now that's what I believe there's always hold no matter what you learn in life if you can unlearn something you can very easily but if you can't that's unfortunate there are some people that cannot differentiate from right or wrong. Those people are falling during the serial killers. And those are the people that owe me in Fantasyland I find those are people with d i d dissociative identy disorder, I have heard of one that had 14 or 24 different personalities and then there was one person that had like 150. 150 personality done one human being has quite a modest but that person went through the same crap I went through only she wasn't as tough as I was I find it's how your brain operations thanks in the Howard deals with life that makes it or breaks it sometimes you end up with schizophrenia sometimes you end up with did sometimes you end up with just playing PTSD or depression it depends on how your brain handles things and how are your maid actually. There are some people with did that are not Psychopaths or anything of the like. But there are some people that look like they have nothing wrong with him I.e my aunt who has something different definitely wrong with them and are manipulative have no emotions have no nothing nothing to offer not even remorse or empathy those are the signs of a psychopath if you let least have d i d PTSD schizophrenia full psychosis or anything of that matter at least you can have some kind of emotion or remorse or empathy but I don't find it with Psychopaths or sociopaths they're not the kind that usually have that and that's what my aunt has that's how I learned from some serial killers through psychology and Psychiatry blocks because I was interested in what was going on and what was making them kick and making them act crazy in the first place actually crazy not mentally ill but crazy so I ended up learning more about serial killers and then I said if you want last year okay with you treat people with more kindness and respect and might help. But then you got people like my Aunt who were completely normal raised not even abused and they are horrible people cure psychopathy I don't even know what she's doing. But that's beside the point I was able to detect a psychopath in her because I was able to watch search serial killer shows when I younger kid. That's when I found that the human emotion and The Human Condition was more important than what was going on in the nice guy as much as the nice guy was beautiful and stress-free and help you understand that your problems are a grain of sand in the beach or desert let's say what really matters is the cause most inside your head that's what's really delicate the cosmos inside your head it can drive you to kill I can drive you to hug and can drive you to do anyting you can or do not want to do it depends on how you are raised how you are wired and other stuff it's very strange and I enjoyed learning about the brain very much so Jesse emotional psychological part. That's why I'm going into mental health one day and why I'm deciding to work with people with trauma so they don't have to do stuff that they don't want to do like kill or hurt people I'm trying to break a stigma that has been annoying to begin with yes there are people like Ted Bundy out there who have been causing a lot of problems and they know they're causing problems and they've had bad experiences in life but then there's also the normal people have the exact same experiences in life and they do not hurt a fly so what is it with the cosmos in the head the mini Cosmos. That's as fascinating as a quasar is an emotion a behaviour of thought is just as interesting as a black hole or a star or the Big Dipper it depends on what you find these interesting if you find Art interesting that's your thing but I find the true cosmos of all this is very interesting that warning the night sky and the one in the head.

It was warned that little obsession with forensic science I got me down this path because I was interested in the car's motion is the brain of a human being that does stupid stuff has been killing people so let's learn about more about the brain and how to take care of it properly and how to take care of a brain properly you raise it probably you treated with kindness and respect that's what I find. I don't think abuse Worth or carrying a homes are very good or broken homes are very good for the human brain in fact there the complete opposite if you are a horrible person that is horrible person meaning you're raised to be evil or wired to be evil. I believe there is hell but it's not in the form of a round or a universe or a Multiverse the same was having it depends on the person you talked to shake hands with the devil shake hands with God is depends on who you are talking to in the first place.

Bruce lees death theory

A lot of idiots believe that Bruce Lee died of this thing called Denmark or the touch of death I don't believe in very much of that. What I think the touch of death has either cyanide or strychnine or succinylcholine. The touch of death it's not a martial arts move that is mythical. That is been the floor and Tibetan and Chinese culture for a long time but it's just been a little or nothing else. What happened to Bruce Lee was he took a pill for a headache and then he never woke up from the headache pill as if it was laced with cyanide that's what I believe and I stick to that to this very day I hear from the martial arts world as damn mark or the toxin death which is not true in fact is the complete opposite it's actually a toxic substance should kill them be a sign out or strychnine I believe something that would kill him quickly in his sleep after he took a pill. He wasn't very saint-like with his life he was very into steroids and stuff I saw it and no one has that kind of body naturally so there could have been someone another bodybuilder who could have been jealous or another martial artist who could have been jealous and wanted it in on whatever he was doing to get himself boss but I've been having this Theory since I was 13 years old that's how smart I am is that I said that Bruce Lee died simply of cyanide or strychnine poisoning cuz he had a seizure or after he took the pill simple symptom of strychnine is the convulsions or seizures whatever you call them but I decide that the touch of death Siri is a pile of crap it's nothing more than yes and this is coming from the girl who believes in everything from the siren head to ghost but I do not believe in the touch of death that is something that is way out of left field no one goes that far no one can be that good at Martial Arts students are you have to poison someone in order to get that effect on someone. That has been my Siri with Bruce Lee as far as I'm concerned that he was poisoned not touched in a certain area that caused him to die you cannot touch someone simply expect them to do I it's not really true or really natural it's not if you were to touch someone to kill them then we'd all be dead it would be a full-on genocide so think about it we use the word touch of death and really isn't or kiss of death it's not really true yeah for me poison in order to have the effect and the publicity to go nuts it has to be poison that killed Bruce Lee I think are nobody thought of that and I was angry at the martial artists who'd go to the Martial Arts Tournament and start talking about the touch of gas and the pressure point I believe in the pressure points cuz I do massages but I don't believe in touch of death I believe in healing people instead I don't really believe too much in martial arts because it's a pile of Mythology to me. Except for the mindfulness part. That part science has actually explain very well and is not junk for the rest of martial arts is Drunk Science and junk everything is not really good except for martial arts or tournaments or self-defense. You can't murder someone with it unless you're really with it and they're very very people are with as I think the last person was very good at martial arts and I was able to kill someone with one touch was in the Han Dynasty and that was two thousand years ago so forget it Bruce Lee died of poison pure and simple just it was so simple. Figure it out but they didn't want to figure it out they wanted to live in la la land

By the time I was thirteen years old when I came up with that theory and then I wanted to be a medical examiner when I was that age before I found out about what mangle a and the other idiots did in World War II instead I now just treasured as particular Theory as a childhood Relic in my brain something that I enjoy to think about sometimes and I tell people from time to time as a conversation starter what do you think Bruce Lee died of if you think Touch of death on a walk away.

I lost so many friends and that obsession with forensic science and wanting to be a medical examiner and all that would I be talking about it since 7th grade to 8th grade..... for a 14 year old or 13 year old when radio was I think was 13 first and then 14 that usually goes as it is in math to the more less try to debunk what the martial artist seek sacred the touch of death and say hello it's poison it was strychnine most likely that killed Bruce Lee that's when I lost all my friends and the martial artist in my school started calling me all those horrible names. And I don't really have very much respect for most martial artists I think they're a bunch of murderers and thieves. I'm not trying to say that the stereotype but I'm just saying that as truth I remember one guy losing a stone precious stone on his Cane and he never got it back and he found it in the dojo of a karate school and he never came back either when he found out when he tried to call the police saying they found his damn stone. So there is a very secretive Society I find very secretive is very shady. And for a 14 year old girl to find this out on her own without even reading a book at the time that is very remarkable. I could write a story about this but I wouldn't want to get kick up any dirt. And start up any more fights with martial artists and get into trouble.

And this is coming from the girl who believe in zombies the Scion had two ghosts and I say this is the first time I lack he said to logic that is not the touch of gas the touch of death is a fictional thing. Take it or leave it. But I know what he died of exactly and I didn't even do the autopsy I was just in a fourteen-year-old girl who happens to know a lot about the world.

Poem of my life

The is a song
A story of a girl

There comes the story
Of a girl
Who was bullied
Out of her mind
Instead of going to recess
She obsessed about collecting
Collecting knowledge
For she step her days
Reading law
Books

There comes the story
The story of a girl
There comes a story
The story of a girl

Still outcast
She sings
And raps
About her feelings
Play your way out
Paint your way out
Write your way out
Sing your way out
Draw your way out
~create your way out
She became the most beautiful
On the inside

There comes a story
A story of a girl
There comes a story
A story of a girl

More like young woman
With light years of experience
Beyond her years
And personality thatis more
Infectious than the cov

There comes a story
A story if a girl
Who just been her self

And was accepted
As is

There was
There was
There was a story
Of a girl
Who became a woman

I was on this site or app called Vent I know that for a fact and I wrote this poem it was supposed to be a song but the song ever was actually approved by a muse but it was under another name. I wanted so much to tell the story about how I came about the Genesis of my own life and this is why I wrote my story out on wordpad. On wordpad I was going to go on the wordy's and try to enter this into the wordy's as well.   If you're wondering what this contest is it's like the Olympics were riding it happens every year around this time June July this time it's around July middle of July the time when I first saw the reanimator HP lovecraft's Re-Animator so I can easily remember it as a 12th I believe on the 21st so I don't remember but I know it was the word ease and I've been Harry I'm very interested in the word ease and wanting to enjoy the contest and actually going to put it off my bucket list that I actually entered for the wordy's.
If I put my mind to it I can write a story with Fifty words or more but I haven't been able to do so very much yet this is my first time and I thought what better story to tell than my own story the story is Sufi me and this is why I had to go and put my own biography so goofy and the actual wordy's competition.   I want to see at least once in my life that I won something or at least competed in something other than Taekwondo and get laughed at for the scientific theory of Bruce Lee's death so that's why I want to go into the word he's so badly that's why I want to win something or attempt to win the wordy's.

This competition has been around for a long time but I only knew about since 2019 around the time of the pandemic that's when I started really writing seriously and that's when I decided I was going to try the word ease but they kept saying oh you have to have 50,000 words try to go into the word pad Hall of Fame their 50,000 words again so I thought the only thing that was worth of 50,000 words with my life so I tell it as it is this is me I am Sufi my interests are stargazing in astronomy I have plenty of other Hang-Ups and interest but those are my two main I'm sessions as well as mental health. I've always had an interest and I'll always stick by my guns and be who I am that's what I'm about being who I am being who you are in the first place not who Society wants you to be or who the martial artist wanted to be but just be yourself be who you are if you want to be a cookie cutter go ahead if you want to be nothing more than a martial artist go ahead but I decide to be Emo goth Punk and that's the end of it. I'm the girl with the pink hair so believe it.

F**k fitting in

Real girls real girls actually keep their clothing on
Real girls have respect for themselves on each other
Real girls don't have sex for fun or money

Think about real girls keep their clothing on and enjoying life as it is
What is the real girl when you think about it
It's your golf girl it's your punk girl it's your EMO girl

Think about what real girls look like
You're either body positive pierced or tattooed never perfectly scanned ever having perfect hips are perfect whatever curves

Think about what a real girl behaves like
Real girls will throw temper tantrums
Real girls will swear
And real girls are determined
Real girls are also meant to be down to earth

Real girls
Real girls
Real girls will spread positivity and happiness by being who they are in the first place
Real girls will wear wigs or different coloured hair they don't have to be blonde

Real girls
Real girls
Real girls don't have perfect boobs or butts
Real girls do not show there anatomy
So keep those clothing on

This is basically a nephew to feeling and because I never believed in fitting and I believe in believing your own stuff and believe in your own person being who you are that's why I wrote this song I was writing this for the album that never came about but I do have 12 albums that didn't come out rap albums under my name sufi but I had other names under the name Melanie Jones Melanie Jones was obviously not going to make it through in the Music World as I did with my actually name. I actually made it on the bottom front which was like music app where you learned to get free music you can go premium if you want but anyway that's beside the point I don't go premium when I listen to modify modify to me is just an outlet for my PTSD when I sleep and also a PTSD Outlet when I'm awake when I laugh PLS on Mike YouTube channel as well and I use for wrap as well and I have eight or nine followers. I'm hoping one day that I can get it as many followers on butterfly and as well as eat true true. That's why I'm working hard at what I do best being myself doing what I want to do rap Hard music maybe get a job one day an actual job get off of disability and end up living a decent life and not have to worry whether I can drive or not I don't care because I don't really care for driving except as a passenger because I tried to drive once and this is funny my father was still holding the steering wheel as he said Sufi gold Take the Wheel I took the wheel I was still in the passenger seat and I ran the car into the neighbor's actual living room that was the end of my driving lesson in my driving career. I never drive again my mom chop it up if he has do you want I was actually diagnosed with the condition finally. She said no white you're not having the driver's license because of their PTSD. And I agreed with her and I stay away from the driver's seat unless I try to turn on the air-conditioning that's why I do that only turn on the air-conditioning on the music other than that I stay away from the drivers China I can just imagine if I wanted to be an airline pilot that that would be gone too because of my PTSD because of one stupid stuff my father pulled there wasn't ptsd-related he did not let go of the wheel instead he just held it until the next thing you know I was trying to refill it out of his hand and the next thing you know we ended up in the neighbours living room and the neighbour was not very happy I remember that neighbour later on being very angry with my father for bringing the ethnic girl into his crafting the ethnic girl into his living room since then he's been aiming fireworks at my parents bedroom window turned out he was a racist how bad was that not only do crash into your cross the street Neighbors living room with it had to be racist at the same time and he ended up whenever there was Canada Victoria Day or New Year's he always threw fireworks in cherry bombs into my parents bedroom window causing them to be awake but mostly I was the one getting annoyed because it is popping sounds and I couldn't stand popping sound yeah I think I'm mostly woke up my parents I think that's what the neighbour warned it is for me to be woken up and piss off my parents while he shoots fireworks and cherry bombs and do it there window so there he was very angry. My father and mother realize it was a neighbour who's living room I crashed into I bet he wasn't too happy but he didn't have to start flowering fireworks in my parents bedroom window just because of my colour of my skin which was ove or to Brown.

Now I don't go driving at all I have the freedom to learn how to drive but I decide not to do it because I'm afraid of crashing into a living room and making another enemy out of that person even though everyone knows I live in a particularly special house and still very risky I don't drive because of my PTSD as well like my mom said because I'd be flipping them the bird all the time me and the middle finger and it would not be a very much your thing when you're trying to pop the kiddy bubble.   So the mature thing for me to do is to never drive except to be in the passenger seat which is the safest place for me. I just say go this way going that way turn here turn there and that's it and I where am I where am where I am and no story. I don't believe in forcing your kids to learn to drive and then having them drive the car near neighbours bloody living room and having a neighbour go get all uptight about racial issues. That was really ridiculous it was what I call rated R rated R meaning the r word. I know there's a lot of people that are rated R and they do not have to be disabled they just help me racist and big ants and dalits and doctors and everything else that I despise in the world that are bad people with disabilities are the people that are the good people that have nothing but goodness in your heart and try to do their life gently and try to do their life in a more positive outlet in fact I don't see any ability or disability I just see a person so really what do you see when you see someone think about a DC colour do you see ability religion or fashion let me tell you I don't see any Jack's shit when I see a person.....just the person.

Authors note

Dear readers and dear judges of the wattys this is a now a gory and a story based on my life as a fictional character but the life events are actually true and true blue I have been through these events in my life on realistically they may seem they are really real to some people unfortunately due to some kids and several countries who haven't been able to make it to a good enough country some of them still live this reality of pain and starvation and horror that is horror and human rights violations and stuff like that there are still many kids we can still see this in the Ukraine chechnya places in Africa there's a lot of places like this where there's a lot of poverty and stuff where kids get abused easily and exploited easily just for the sake of it or because of religion to say. I know I should be careful of what I say here but this is what it is I was abused in the name of religion extremist religion that is not just any religion but extremist religion and I was also abused by the Catholic religion trying to be is assimilated because I was also non-binary lesbian and I'm different race whatever a races. So this is just an allegory and a a fictional version of my autobiography which tells of many things I hope this has a lot of takeaways to people that you have to feed other people with respect and kindness that you have to treat other people and not touch other people in harming or sexual manner unless you want they want you to do but I don't think they want you to so don't bother. I believe that it's important to be kind and respectful and think of other people and give back to the world so don't even bother ruining it for anyone else wear your mask if you have to if it's covid and if it isn't covid-19 just at least be a decent person or at least stay home if you're going to spread hatred cuz hatred is the worst pandemic there is on the planet then at least we can cure or try to kill her the covid-19 but there is no cure for hatred and terrorism and War there is that still rampant all over the world it is a pandemic that the medical community cannot fix. The only way to fix it is for people like me to expose it as it is a disease a hatred that is needed most me for no reason but I hate other people for different colour or different religion or politics or orientation instead let's try to spread the love love is more contagious I find love I mean love is more and acceptance is more contagious and more accepting and give me more powerful weapon against hatred war and violence and terrorism then there is with page two wrongs do not make a right if you are going to not have anything nice to say just like with covid stay the hell home don't even bother that's the takeaway of this is that you don't bother other people while they're trying to have a decent lifo anyway you people be and let them enjoy their lies and peace that's what it's about do not try to judge people because that'll just make them better than you and you just nothing more than a virus particle. Which would be a smidgen of an existence so think about this when you say something stupid to someone or you call someone a mean name that you're dressed diminishing yourself in your existence are you going to become a cockroach are you going to become something less than a human no but you're just going to look like a ruddy fool and I mean why diminish Your Existence so think about it try to think about how you treat other people how you treat babies is really important if you treat a baby correctly and properly and kindly the baby will not remember a thing but if you treat the baby horribly most likely they're going to remember every second of it. Ended doesn't have to be someone with PTSD it just means someone with some sort of trauma in childhood you have for treat children with the respect that they deserve like gold. And I even know of one neighbour who even throughout her kids when they were 18 years old because they were 18 years old and she didn't want to have to deal with them. So I ended up saying that's not what humans do either like this year old killer is we can learn from our mistakes and learn not to act a fool or a criminal or an active serial killer we can actually learn to behave properly and move forward this is why I told my story so people can understand if they can understand the story that it's important to be polite and kind and caring and decent human being and compassionate. Do not try to talk someone in the mouth they might remember it for the rest of their life is very true I remember everything that I've went through good and bad. And this is just my fictional autobiography Sufi is just a character that I came up with. I hope you enjoyed the book and I hope this makes it to the wattys.

The story of Susie Isabel more or less any kid that has been abused in anyway and has stood up for themselves or sought help in anyway I sought help through God he was able to send whatever Anthony to my mother to make her aware of my presence in this world and was able to give her the ability to adopt me from my idiot one And idiot to family, really my birth mother was the sanction was resolved and there was many women in Romania at the time under those idiots rule that it was a government sanction rape and there's got government sanctioned terrorism just like in Iran with government sanctioned terrorism but now I do not demonize Iran because I have penpals in Iran as well as I don't demonize any other country but I don't like Romania particularly because of what happened to me but anyway I was a victim of torture in the product of rape when I found out about the right part I was a little spooked I didn't say that in the story but that's what my brother had told me one day and I was a little freaked out by it and it was a little scary but it's part of my story it's part of Sufi stories part of the book there are many women in Romania that have been abused by the government just to have children and when they find out that their girls end of either during the wrong abortions or they end up killing the kid or adopting kid out usually adopting the kid it would mean certain death as well because a kid would be in an orphanage and would be tortured by Al-Qaeda which is not very pleasant to think about when you're reading the waters you want to read a nice one story which is kind of a fun story but there is an allegory to her this is my life story and I want to be able to tell it as it is but this is what it happened in my life my first two years of my life and one followed through afterwords. This is why I've written Sufi a novel. Sufi is based on my personality and my character as well as my own human body she also has a swearing water molecule tattoo a Jupiter tat two and two semicolon tattoos what she learned earned I mean from an online course he took for a suicide prevention then she ended up learning more wanting to learn more about the human mind do you know cosmos hasn't called and then she wanted to learn it freely without the cost she had it up getting the help from my guy I'm not gonna say his name because of confidentiality but he actually helped me get hooked up to some social work courses that are free and me is going to be able be able to help myself as well as the other people around me the people that want help at least the people that don't want help well I can't really do very much but the people that want help or that needed the most will get it from me. I'm not always a rough and tough tumbling kinda girl. I as I said I have a smart side as sensitive side but I also have a very tough side to myself as well because of my time in Catholic school it was eat or be eaten like prison. And that is no joke you had to survive to live another day to get to bed at night that was what Catholic school was like that was what Catholic school was like for me and Leticia Leticia was a girl I knew from high school she also had a fight tooth and nail just go to bed at night to almost 3 victim of bullycide herself school sanctioned bullycide I should say.

It is important to teach our kids the importance of not bullying and that bullying can cause a lot of problems and complications in a persons life as well as PTSD can become morbid PTSD or complex PTSD I happen to have comorbid and complex PTSD which a cameramen was from my time in Romania being born and then being thrown away like a piece of garbage and then being treated like a piece of garbage until I was two years old two months and then the complex PTSD was from my time in Catholic school and nearly dying of bullycide which is suicide through bullying more or less it's like murder through bullying you killed a person through suicide is not very pleasant I want to make this very where do people this is an original story that people need to know this I hope will made the warranty so I don't know. But I do hope that it reaches someone that needs some kind of help if it doesn't make the worries at least please let this book help somebody there's a need of some positivity or guidance or some thing this is why I decided to write this book because it so many kids die from bullying or they drop out of school and become homeless because of bullying and other complications in their lives and I just think as a moral society it's just terrible. This is why I wrote a book because I read about and Warren about youth reconnect and I wanted to more or less tell my bit of the side of my story of what nearly cost me my home and my shelter as well as also my mental health. This is what my life was and some of it may seem unbelievable and on real this is what it is this is my 33 years on this planet like it or Lampert that's the way it goes with life you either believe it or you don't what are you believe the siren head or the UFOs that's on you but I believe in them personally but as I said this is about my life how it got complex in the first place very first place and I did up becoming something a little bit better in the end and hopefully my next 66 years or 100 years would be a lot better depending on what God has planned for me and I don't know what that is just yet. I hope you enjoy the book I know it's some of it may be disturbing solve it far-fetched but it's true And clear as the word fuck now you cannot deny that word you can deny hearing it but you cannot do know that it was sad think about it.

Dear readers and dear judges of the wattys this is a now a gory and a story based on my life as a fictional character but the life events are actually true and true blue I have been through these events in my life on realistically they may seem they are really real to some people unfortunately due to some kids and several countries who haven't been able to make it to a good enough country some of them still live this reality of pain and starvation and horror that is horror and human rights violations and stuff like that there are still many kids we can still see this in the Ukraine chechnya places in Africa there's a lot of places like this where there's a lot of poverty and stuff where kids get abused easily and exploited easily just for the sake of it or because of religion to say. I know I should be careful of what I say here but this is what it is I was abused in the name of religion extremist religion that is not just any religion but extremist religion and I was also abused by the Catholic religion trying to be is assimilated because I was also non-binary lesbian and I'm different race whatever a races. So this is just an allegory and a a fictional version of my autobiography which tells of many things I hope this has a lot of takeaways to people that you have to feed other people with respect and kindness that you have to treat other people and not touch other people in harming or sexual manner unless you want they want you to do but I don't think they want you to so don't bother. I believe that it's important to be kind and respectful and think of other people and give back to the world so don't even bother ruining it for anyone else wear your mask if you have to if it's covid and if it isn't covid-19 just at least be a decent person or at least stay home if you're going to spread hatred cuz hatred is the worst pandemic there is on the planet then at least we can cure or try to kill her thc covid-19 but there is no cure for hatred and terrorism and War there is that still rampant all over the world it is a pandemic that the medical community cannot fix. The only way to fix it is for people like me to expose it as it is a disease a hatred that is needed most me for no reason but I hate other people for different colour or different religion or politics or orientation instead let's try to spread the love love is more contagious I find love I mean love is more and acceptance is more contagious and more accepting and give me more powerful weapon against hatred war and violence and terrorism then there is with page two wrongs do not make a right if you are going to not have anything nice to say just like with covid stay the hell home don't even bother that's the takeaway of this is that you don't bother other people while they're trying to have a decent life anyway you people be and let them enjoy their lies and peace that's what it's about do not try to judge people because that'll just make them better than you and you just nothing more than a virus particle. Which would be a smidgen of an existence so think about this when you say something stupid to someone or you call someone a mean name that you're dressed diminishing yourself in your existence are you going to become a cockroach are you going to become something less than a human no but you're just going to look like a ruddy fool and I mean why diminish Your Existence so think about it try to think about how you treat other people how you treat babies is really important if you

treat a baby correctly and properly and kindly the baby will not remember a thing but if you treat the baby horribly most likely they're going to remember every second of it. Ended doesn't have to be someone with PTSD it just means someone with some sort of trauma in childhood you have for treat children with the respect that they deserve like gold. And I even know of one neighbour who even throughout her kids when they were 18 years old because they were 18 years old and she didn't want to have to deal with them. So I ended up saying that's not what humans do either like this year old killer is we can learn from our mistakes and learn not to act a fool or a criminal or an active serial killer we can actually learn to behave properly and move forward this is why I told my story so people can understand if they can understand the story that it's important to be polite and kind and caring and decent human being and compassionate. Do not try to talk someone in the mouth they might remember it for the rest of their life is very true I remember everything that I've went through good and bad. And this is just my fictional autobiography Sufi is just a character that I came up with. I hope you enjoyed the book and I hope this makes it to the wattys.
The story of Sufi Mustafa a more or less any kid that has been abused in anyway and has stood up for themselves or sought help in anyway I sought help through God he was able to send whatever Anthony to my mother to make her aware of my presence in this world and was able to give her the ability to adopt me from my idiot one And idiot to family, really my birth mother was the sanction was resolved and there was many women in Romania at the time under those idiots rule that it was a government sanction rape and there's got government sanctioned terrorism just like in Iran with government sanctioned terrorism but now I do not demonize Iran because I have penpals in Iran as well as I don't demonize any other country but I don't like Romania particularly because of what happened to me but anyway I was a victim of torture in the product of rape when I found out about the right part I was a little spooked I didn't say that in the story but that's what my brother had told me one day and I was a little freaked out by it and it was a little scary but it's part of my story it's part of Sufi stories part of the book there are many women in Romania that have been abused by the government just to have children and when they find out that their girls end of either during the wrong abortions or they end up killing the kid or adopting kid out usually adopting the kid it would mean certain death as well because a kid would be in an orphanage and would be tortured by Al-Qaeda which is not very pleasant to think about when you're reading the waters you want to read a nice one story which is kind of a fun story but there is an allegory to her this is my life story and I want to be able to tell it as it is but this is what it happened in my life my first two years of my life and one followed through afterwords. This is why I've written Sufi a novel.   Sufi is based on my personality and my character as well as my own human body she also has a swearing water molecule tattoo a Jupiter tat two and two semicolon tattoos what she learned earned I mean from an online course he took for a suicide prevention then she ended up learning more wanting to learn more about the human mind do you know cosmos hasn't called and then she wanted to learn it freely without the cost she had it up getting the help from my guy I'm not gonna say his name because of confidentiality but he actually helped me get hooked up to some social work courses that are free and me is going to be able be able to help myself as well as the other people around me the people that want help at least the people that don't want help well I can't really do very much but the people that want help or that needed the most will get it from me. I'm not always a rough and tough tumbling kinda girl. I as I said I have a smart side as sensitive side but I also have a very tough side to myself as well because of my time in Catholic school it was eat or be eaten like prison. And that is no joke you had to survive to live another day to get to bed at night that was what Catholic school was like that was what Catholic school was like for me and Leticia Leticia was a girl I knew from high school she also had a fight tooth and nail just go to bed at night to almost 3 victim of bullycide herself school sanctioned bullycide I should say.
It is important to teach our kids the importance of not bullying and that bullying can cause a lot of problems and complications in a persons life as well as PTSD can

become morbid PTSD or complex PTSD I happen to have comorbid and complex PTSD which a cameramen was from my time in Romania being born and then being thrown away like a piece of garbage and then being treated like a piece of garbage until I was two years old two months and then the complex PTSD was from my time in Catholic school and nearly dying of bullycide which is suicide through bullying more or less it's like murder through bullying you killed a person through suicide is not very pleasant I want to make this very where do people this is an original story that people need to know this I hope will made the warranty so I don't know. But I do hope that it reaches someone that needs some kind of help if it doesn't make the worries at least please let this book help somebody there's a need of some positivity or guidance or some thing this is why I decided to write this book because it so many kids die from bullying or they drop out of school and become homeless because of bullying and other complications in their lives and I just think as a moral society it's just terrible. This is why I wrote a book because I read about and Warren about youth reconnect and I wanted to more or less tell my bit of the side of my story of what nearly cost me my home and my shelter as well as also my mental health. This is what my life was and some of it may seem unbelievable and on real this is what it is this is my 33 years on this planet like it or Lampert that's the way it goes with life you either believe it or you don't what are you believe the siren head or the UFOs that's on you but I believe in them personally but as I said this is about my life how it got complex in the first place very first place and I did up becoming something a little bit better in the end and hopefully my next 66 years or 100 years would be a lot better depending on what God has planned for me and I don't know what that is just yet. I hope you enjoy the book I know it's some of it may be disturbing solve it far-fetched but it's true And clear as the word fuck now you cannot deny that word you can deny hearing it but you cannot do know that it was sad think about it.

I hope you can accept Sophie as you can accept who I am as well Sophia is who I am this is not DID or dissociative identity disorder this is just a fictional character based on myself who I believe is right in the world who has done nothing wrong but is he a saint no is he a Buddha no but she is a human being that needs respect and kindness and recognition and that's why I wrote the book to show that Sophic or myself needs to be respected with the most respect and kindness like every other human being we are expected to be kind to everyone but as soon as we see someone who is different we get fucked in the face right away particularly if we are the unique person in that way and I chose never to be the same as everyone else I thought that would be boring of a life and I decide to be nothing more than to be human unique artistic musical creative and literary instead that help me through a lot of my problems in my life and help me survive my childhood moles early and middle to late childhood. And even help me through my 20s to help me create instead of destroy stuff and if I did destroy stuff and I know I did because I was angry person in the 20s are using broken stuff as artwork kind of like a part with golden glue to fill in the cracks I use the broken stuff that I broke in my flashbacks or rages and I use them in my photography and that's what I did I made something beautiful out of something I made destructive instead of making it seem sad and disappointing and saying I'll fuck I broke something I said oh fuck just like my three earlobes I just said well it's just the way it is. So I end up deciding that to write this park because that's what my life is it was something broken I want to put it back together and tell my story and which is a Sufi story a fictional character based on me

You're probably where I come up with my stories about my life but they are actually true advance with the weather be Bruce Lee's death theory or the cheating boyfriend or half the stuff that I went through or the ghost dog it's true I've been through it I've said it it's been what it was I've seen it been there done it you know that saying and that's how I come up with half the stuff in my horror stories two is half the stuff that I go through in my life. I'm more or less trying to say what who I am through this book and what my stories about which is not just a story about pain but about beauty as well

Just get back read the book and enjoy the story and I hope you don't get too horrified with my beginnings as I was horrified with my beginnings but I wasn't horrified afterwards and when I found out these clowns were just clowns that hurt women and children well as 3000 people we also have to think about not just the living victims of terrorism at the 3000 people and the dead victims of terrorism who haven't made it I know that sound a little not so tactful but we have to think about the deceased victims of terrorism as well as the real live victims of terrorism and vice versa. Whether living or dead a victim of terrorism deserves to be honoured not as a victim but I was a survivor not even a survivor but I Thriver and a helper of humanity do exposure Gradyville that's why I've been put on this planet in the way and why I was put to put this book together within 24 hours practically I know that that's a little ridiculous 50 000 words in 24 hours but that is basically what I have to deal with because I am very creative and I have a lot of ideas because I have a lot of stuff that goes on in my life that I enjoy very much and sometimes not enjoy

Sufi Mustafa is my rapper name Sufi Spraggah bint Mustafa, that is my rapper name and I just happen to use that as inspiration for my character's name Sofi who is a pink haired girl who wears pink wigs who likes to help people and tries to help people but sometimes the fumbles that I told you just read the story you will get the gist of it right away just think about. Other people in the unreasonable ways other people treat them which is why I think we are treat people more kindly it is on real how other people treat others for the race religion ass near city or whatever or whatever kind of DNA that they have more whatever it is it's the same DNA we have the same from mom the same from dad and that's the same thing 23 from both parents 46 chromosomes unless we have a medical condition that says otherwise even at that we're still human with the medical condition that might have a micro deletion or a deletion or whatever in a gene that might cause a missing chromosome Eleonora extra chromosome but that doesn't take away that we're only human. Human is how we treat each other humans what this is the take away what is human. Really humans about being randomly kind and caring and decent human person. We throw this word human as in for humanoids and people but really human is a state of mind it's not a scientific term for a species if we are a species we are a good species of good people who will treat each other with kindness and respect that's what human is treating others with kindness and respect not killing each other not ostracize each other or anything else to that fact that might bring a negative affect on another person a human will treat each other with respect and kindness and protect each other think about it tell me what your idea of human years is it just a genetic group of animals or is that really what it really is a state of mind trying to help other people. What I want you to take away with this book is very simple that human is not a species or an animal it's a way of life it's just trying to be a human being is not trying to be us unless ascetic but trying to be a person trying to live a good decent life trying to help other people. Trying to be creative trying to not be destructive. Try not to be self-destructive I remember all the time still and I still to this day see in my living room in my group home the sign behind your self and then if you would be kind to yourself you'll be kind to others as well it's a lot easier and you'll be a lot quicker that way and a lot less painful and more human to be kinder to yourself into other people as well think about it that's the take away. Like there were a lot of people that I don't think were very kind to themselves because they weren't kind to me in return. Instead they ended up getting a whole pile of bullshit back from me instead of being getting kindness they end up getting bullshit from me because they gave bullshit because they gave them selves bullshit instead of trying to help themselves or trying to be kind to themselves that would really go miles around the world just being kind to yourself and then then just helping yourself and then you can help other people and be kind to other people use your head people. That's what the take away is just be kind to everyone including yourself I was always kind of myself in the story even though I did stupid stunts. What I want you to know is to be entertained but not horrified by the story but also informed and entertained and do actually be provolked into thought. That's why I wrote the story this is why I have this life that I live it's a thought-provoking life it's the life that makes people think should I live a better life should I live more decent life should I learn more should I better myself like this Sufi girl think about it I just want you to think about this read I should've said read this before you read the actual book but besides the point this is the end of the book I hope you enjoyed it I hope you didn't get too horrified by it I know this is the longest part of the Epologue. The beginning and the end of a book has the most boring part of the book I find the juicy parts are usually the stuff that you find in the middle of the book it's the journey not the destination and certainly not the beginning.

Jamila Nujuum

Ps: If you confronted with Comcast like the warranties for example where are you have to go and Paul 50000 words out of your butt might I suggest a challenge that you use your life and life experience in life experience as a way of telling a story as an inspiration for the next book for the Wadd think about it use your life as the story that must be told it is the story that must be told think about it the next time you go and do a riding contest let's say like the walkies or the whatever involves the 50,000 word limit you have to think with your mind but don't do something that you don't know that is fictional use your mind and think with your heart is your life as a story think about it and it might unlock some thing you never know you don't know unless you try this is my challenge when you go to the wattys do you use your life as a template and union life experience as a template for your story no matter how horrible go today is your life or how boring or interesting use your life as a template for your next block for the wattys I dare you to try that. Cause they say in the war is you have a story that needs to be told and really what's the biggest story that needs to be told but the story that's far of your life so next year when you come to the wattys is try to think of this book and try to think maybe I'm going to use my life experience in life trauma or drama or life happy nurses as a template for my book for the next wattys think about it or the next whatever. But then again I'm not someone who works for Wattpad I just write on Wattpad I just tell things as it is just be truthful about it being take it from the heart and you will win whatever contest you enter I don't make the rules as I said I just use the app. And I just enter the contest just like you but I'm just giving you this is my book take it run with it maybe you can use it for your own advantage your life use that as your next big story for the wattys or the next big contest on Wattpad think about it just use your life as a template use the characters as the people that are in your life give them fictional names and think about it for a while but you have to have the right kind of inspiration my inspiration came from getting my first certification in social work which was the youth reconnect. I talk what my friend gave me which was free online courses and I use that as a template and the strength to tell about my end of the story on how bad life can get but also how good life can get at some points I remember two kids in my neighbourhood who were kicked out of his their house right when they were 18 or 17 because they were 17 or 18 they had nowhere to go they were more or less homeless MOS screw blowed and tattooed and they had to go and sign one of them had to go to a shelter the other two friends boyfriends mothers place I remember that correctly but they never made it in life one trying to be a cop the other try to be an artist it wasn't very easy for them their life wasn't hard but it wasn't easy for them either they weren't very homeless either like the people in my courses. The girl which is Anna Anna means mother and Uighur ended up getting a few tattoos but she didn't get very much in life except for those tattoos nails the guy never got very far and it was the royal screwup and ruined his hygiene which is a real risk factor for men many things is a fucked up hygiene. That's basically my life and these were my friends at one point until they were kicked out of their own home because of the rage their age and that was simple as that I was never kicked out because of my age or my orientation on my religion I was just kicked I kick myself out because I thought the place was toxic at the time. Where in one person was in or two people were in a toxic home environment all their lives I was never gonna ttoxic home environment but I was gonna toxic school environment, what you added to my PTSD the other people had a toxic home life they never really enjoyed their life they had to go to school in order to enjoy life and they had to be on the upper levels of school like the the popular kids or they were told show it wasn't very fun for them I didn't have to and I didn't want to fight and because I didn't have to worry about being kicked out I don't know early age. I but I do try to use Your life and your life experience as a template for your next novel or wattys work think about it it might work. I was just lucky I had a very exciting horrifying but good and annoying life at the same time it had many layers like an onion so try to see if you can find your layers in your onion of life and try to write about it in the next warranties next year try that for an example I'm not trying to say anything I'm just trying to say this is what I'm doing maybe this might be something that might help you in the future when you do the wattys. When you decide to do the wattys it's not a light task to do 50,000 words in fact I spent the whole day blabbering away on the microphone trying to scroungo up every single memory that I can think of it was very intense. I am very lucky that it's it took the day away for me so I didn't have to deal with the day but anyways it was very interesting to make it up to 49,000 words or not I'm sure I'm sure I'm up to the 50 I don't know we'll see but try T what I'm saying is declined other people one and also if you can I use your life as a template for your next book for Wattpad go for it that's what I did for the wattys for this year and I might do the same again next year who the hell knows. I'm just giving that says I think PS post script as a suggestion.

www.ingramcontent.com/pod-product-compliance
Lightning Source LLC
LaVergne TN
LVHW052054160826
845678LV00015B/3230

* 9 7 9 8 8 3 8 4 3 0 9 6 0 *